Mall

Eric Bogosian

Mall

A NOVEL

SIMON & SCHUSTER

New York   London   Toronto   Sydney   Singapore

SIMON & SCHUSTER
Rockefeller Center
1230 Avenue of the Americas
New York, NY 10020

Simon & Schuster and colophon are registered trademarks
of Simon & Schuster, Inc.

Designed by Katy Riegel
Manufactured in the United States of America
1 3 5 7 9 10 8 6 4 2

Library of Congress Cataloging-in-Publication Data
Bogosian, Eric.
Mall : a novel / Eric Bogosian.
p. cm.
1. Shopping malls—Fiction. 2. Narcotic addicts—Fiction. 3. Young men—Fiction.
4. Violence—Fiction. I. Title.
PS3552.O46 M35 2000
813'.54—dc21
00-057331

ISBN 0-684-85727-8
ISBN 0-7432-0353-4 (signed edition)

For Harry and Travis

Mall

I'm frightened by the devil and I'm drawn to those ones that ain't afraid.

Joni Mitchell, "A Case of You"

No avoiding it: life does want death. To be alive is to kill.

John Updike, *Rabbit Redux*

1

"MAL!" Mary's voice cut like an airhorn through the aging ranch house. Past the framed needlepoint-by-numbers, past the mute upright piano, past the dusty royal blue–and–gold *Encyclopedia Americana,* past the dripping bathroom faucet, over the wall-to-wall rugs flat with beaten paths, past the circa-1962 pole lamp, down the dark hallway, under the door of the TV den and into Mal's ear.

"Malcolm! You want your dinner now?"

Mal was as still as a lizard on a warm rock, pupils dilated, absorbing the TV images across the close air of the darkened room.

Mal knew how concerned his mother was regarding his relationship with food. She had discussed his problem with the doctors and the therapists and they had informed her that one way to tell if Mal was abusing any mood elevators was if he had no appetite or if he was particularly active. Clutching this inside information close to her chest Mary felt she had the upper hand. But Mal knew something neither his mom nor the doctors knew: A) if necessary, he could force himself to eat; and B) sometimes when he was speeding on crystal meth he didn't move at all. Instead he directed all his energy into his thoughts and became pure consciousness. Which was what he had been doing for the past three months. Mary thought he had been watching TV or sleeping. But she was wrong. For ninety days, Mal had been thinking and planning, his thoughts as convoluted as a fever patient's nightmare.

Even now, Mal jammed one more conceptual log into the inferno of his brainpan, a memory. The tan brick church embraced by its tiny lawn; the bone white Mary weeping over bloody geraniums; the darkly shellacked doors agape. Inside the cool, frankincense-infused building, Father Donleavy, no, Father Donahue, no, Father Donavon, no, Father Fuckface, that's it, Father Fuckface with the scraped-red cheekskin, is blabbing: Jesus said this and Jesus said that.

And Jesus said, "Why do you kick against the pricks?" And the sullen twelve-year-old Malcolm, his butt perched on the smooth rock-hard oak pew, responds impiously: "But I don't. I don't. I want the pricks *and* the kicks." Another image replaces the questioning Jesus of Nazareth in the fever swirl of Mal's sweaty mind—a tiny bird, swooping quickly. The bird hits the windshield, fragments into fluff and blood, then gets swallowed up by blackness.

"I'm making fish sticks with mashed potatoes and string beans. Okay?"

Surrounded by the dull food smell of meals past, Mary peered into the oven. The mini-lightbulb inside, covered with black oven grease-goo, hid in its corner, cold and dead. Asking Mal to repair something was futile. There were times when he would get very busy and excited, but instead of doing anything constructive, Mal would only create more confusion. Tools and bits of broken litter would end up strewn all over the living room rug. And guess who had to clean all that up? So Mary lived with the dead light-bulb and the withered mouse carcasses in the basement and the dripping bathroom faucet with its green stain printed onto the black-chipped porcelain.

Mary tugged the tray of fish sticks to see if they had the ap-propriate brown tinge. The hot metal tilted and dropped. It painted her thumb with a fiery smear of pain. She juggled the whole business, trying to keep the little oily loaves from skidding onto the floor, only to get seared again.

She could put butter on the wounds later. Her immediate mis-sion was to feed and nurture Mal. Sam was dead, Traci was gone, but there was still little Malcolm. Not so little and childlike now with his beard and stringy hair and fog of B.O. She wished she could toss him into the tub like when he was six. Well, "one step at a time" as it said in the magazine.

Mary slid the fish sticks onto a cheery patterned plate. She scooped mashed potatoes, dabbed butter and forked on the boiled, canned string beans. Canned were better. They tasted ter-rible, but Mal never noticed the difference and they were cheaper. She set the food, fork and knife, salt and pepper, a slice of bread on a smaller matching plate and a flimsy paper napkin on a tray, snapped off the oven and made her way down the hall to the TV room. She noticed the mute piano and made a mental note to wipe it down with Pledge in the morning.

Entering the darkened room, Mary searched for the TV table upon which Mal customarily took his meals. She ignored the slight scent of urine. Mal did not move, the TV set murmured.

"Did you hear me calling you?"

Mal did not speak.

"Well, if you're not going to tell me what you want or don't want, I'm going to make your decisions for you and you're going to get what you get. The older you are the more you remind me of your father."

Mal scratched under his armpit and looked up at his mother. His eyes shone crystalline blue, numinous in the reflected light of the TV. Underneath it all, he was a handsome man. With the beard and hair he looked almost like Our Savior Himself. Mary loved him. She put the tray down.

"There. You need anything else? You want me to get you a Hi-C?"

Mal eyed the tray. Eyed Mary. He lay the remote control upon the armrest, reached under his greasy, lumpy BarcaLounger seat cushion and extracted a vague shape in the semidarkness.

"What's that, Mal?"

Mal straightened his arm toward his mother's chest as if he were going to accuse her of something, as if she had done something wrong. He didn't speak. He merely moved his finger a quarter of an inch. The little .22 semiautomatic made a *bang* sound like a big cap pistol. Mary looked down but there wasn't anything to see. She felt a burning, then realized Mal had shot her.

"Did you just do what I think you did, Mal?"

Mary finished the sentence as her lungs collapsed and her tightly coiled energy unwound. She decided the fish sticks on the plate needed adjusting. She reached out to touch them, but her body wasn't doing anything it was supposed to. Mary watched the plate come up and hit her in the face. Mary, the plate, the tray and the TV table crashed into the BarcaLounger. Mary found herself folded in half, the green and ochre food staining her and the floor. She looked up at her son, still sitting in the naugahyde recliner.

"Mal? Now who's going to clean this up?" She coughed and a small pink bubble inflated out of her left nostril.

Mal put the gun to her forehead and squeezed off a second round. It smacked Mary backward. The bullet didn't penetrate her skull, rather skidded off toward a shelf where a crystal glass memorializing Traci's wedding stood, shattering it, filling the air with a mini-snowstorm of glass particles. Mary was scurrying toward the door like a broken crab.

Mal watched her with the same dim interest with which he watched his TV. She did not die the way the dogs had died. Dogs bite at the wound like a bad flea because they don't know what's going on. Mary knew. She had no more questions for Mal. She knew the doctor was wrong in his diagnosis. Mal was not better.

2

The summer air hung heavy with molecular bits of exhaust and humidity. Dusk consumed the suburbs: the roadways, the houses, the mall. As each portion was digested, a new glowing entity arose. The streaming red and white of the highway encircled the gold and TV blue of the picture windows. The acidic orange of excited mercury vapor bloomed over the parking lots.

Jeff sat erect in full lotus on a patch of clipped turf demarked on one side by a short, heavy-duty guardrail and on the other by a sloping grade of asphalt that flattened downward and out to form the east side of the shopping mall parking lot. His rigid posture was a foil for his dripping dreadlocks and ragged clothing.

Cars and light trucks, thumping with muffled music, swished past or braked in syncopation to the traffic light a hundred yards up by the entrance to the mall. Jeff closed his eyes and meditated on the chirp of dusty brake pads and the hum of the interstate a quarter mile away. He reached up and touched one of his dirty blond dreads, twisting it 'round his finger.

Jeff raised as much interest as a fire hydrant. Occasionally, a mask of a face would target him, but through the safety glass there was no contact. An antic child waved to no one in particular. Jeff returned the wave and the kid rolled his eyes and flopped out of sight like a spaz.

Jeff cleared his head, tried not to think about Adelle. He focused his Buddha-mind upon the surface where he sat. This grass was not normal grass. It was some sort of heavy-duty polluted crabgrass. Opaque plastic lids from fast-food drink cups, dull ersatz cork cigarette filters, string and exhaust-darkened sand collected here. Down the way, a discarded oil filter lay on its side bleeding sludge.

Jeff could lie down and make a camp here and no one would see him or bother him. He could live here for years, panhandling the cars stopped at the light, jogging down to the Burger King for a quick snack. He could read every book in existence. People would throw them to him from the windows of cars. He would exist off the grid, a modern Thoreau, never having to kowtow to authority or play in the bullshit of the corporate hurly-burly. He could write a journal and someday, when he died, his journal would be discovered and the world would realize that the stranger by the road was no mere mortal but a sensitive genius who scribbled wisdom as they flew past in their brutish vehicles.

As if he had willed its appearance, a police cruiser quietly rolled to a stop before Jeff's spot. This time, the people inside were looking at him and did see him.

"How we doin' tonight?"

Jeff weighed his options. He could answer the cop as if the cop were actually talking to him (rather than a preconceived notion of who he was) or he could "goof."

"You gonna answer me?"

Jeff remained mute and a second cop reluctantly popped his door and swung out from the shotgun seat. He ambled slowly around the rear bumper of the cruiser and, hand on gun butt, stood before Jeff. This guy had a blond instead of dark brown mustache. He began with a slow easy tone of voice.

"So how we doin' here?"

"Fine."

"What's your name?"

"Why are you touching your gun? Are you planning to shoot me?"

The cop loosened a shoulder, then a hip. "Not tonight. You on drugs?"

"No, I am not on drugs."

"You hitchhiking?"

"That's how I got here."

"So what's going on?"

"I don't have to tell you that. I'm sitting here."

"Uh-huh. What are you? Eighteen? Nineteen?"

Jeff said nothing. The cop with the blond mustache squatted down so his eyes were level with Jeff's. He brought his face close, his smile as synthetic as his shirt. His irises were clear green.

"You don't have to talk to me. You're right about that. On the other hand, I have a job to do. I don't think you mean to cause trouble, but that's what you're doing. What if someone in a passing vehicle looks over and gets in an accident 'cause of you? Would you like that? What if a bumper got bumped? Or, God forbid, a child got hurt? Maybe taken to the hospital?"

"That would never happen."

"I've seen a lot of things that would never happen, happen."

"I could sit here for a thousand years and I wouldn't be hurting a soul."

The cool green eyes grew cooler. "This is private property, son. Unless you have business here, you have to leave."

"This isn't private property."

"It is. It belongs to the mall. Everything around here belongs to the mall. The roadway too. Hey, I don't like it any more than you do."

"If you don't like it, why are you protecting it?"

"Come on, man. Get your shit together. You don't want to get busted, you *know* you don't. Tell you what, I'll drive you down to the Sears."

The cop spoke to Jeff in the universal hip language. Everyone was cool these days. Jeff felt the power of the machine bearing down on him.

"So you want to do that?"

"What?" Jeff pulled one of his dreads. He scratched his nose.

The cop glanced back at his partner in the cruiser. "You want us to give you a lift down to the mall?"

"I'll move. I'm moving," Jeff said, slowly rising.

"Thanks."

"I think it's sad." Jeff's smooth face darkened.

"What's sad?"

"That people like you are brainwashed by some corporate machine to dehumanize yourselves by dehumanizing others. And it's sad that a person can't just sit down where he wants."

"You can sit down, pal. You just can't sit down here. Sorry."

The cop got back in the cruiser and shared a few inaudible words and a sharp laugh. The car rolled off.

Jeff didn't take a step. He watched the cops watching him from their rearview mirror as they waited in line at the traffic light. In those two seconds, thoughts flashed through Jeff's mind. Thoughts about humans and animals and consciousness and unconsciousness and fascism and revolution and the frustration of having insight when you are surrounded by the narrow-minded. As the light turned green and the line of cars slipped forward, the police cruiser stood waiting. Only then did Jeff take a step.

Jeff made his way down the embankment, wading into a metallic sea of shiny Camrys and Malibus and Broncos. He crossed the black plain of asphalt, the recycled rubber of his faux-Tevas crunching bits of broken glass and grit. Confused bugs looped above in the artificial light. Heat clung to the breezeless flatland, unable to rise into the darkening air. The perpetual interstate traffic droned over Jeff's shoulder—larger insects returning to their respective hives. Darkness was falling slowly, yet things were getting brighter in a way.

Jeff avoided the doors where the food court guarded the entrance to the mall. His group of chums would be there, balling soda straw sheaths, tipping waxy cups back, crunching ice between slack jaws. They'd be talking shit, flirting, torturing one another, their bad posture daring the guard to force them to move. The mall had no use for lounging, no use for them.

Adelle would be there. Not saying much, almost pouting. Her blonde-tangerine hair in her eyes, arms limp, legs akimbo. Jeff interpreted her ennui as a kind of efficiency, a kind of wisdom. "She's full of life, but she's saving it for the right moment, for the right one." An older guy, from another town, had been taking Adelle to places none of Jeff and his friends had access to. When this older guy had found her too young and boring, he had abandoned her. Jeff intuited that when Adelle came back to the old gang, she considered it the booby prize for being unlucky in love.

Jeff wanted to sit near Adelle and inhale the perfume of her pale, freckled skin. He wanted to share her dark, depressed state of mind. She was not insubstantial like the rest of them, Adelle had gravity, she understood how thickly and sadly the world coursed. But by going and sitting with her, by being near her, he would automatically become one of the jokers and nothing more. Jeff thought, Beckett said show up at nine, it's nine now, so he took his time.

He made his way along the stuccoed gray walls, the outer skin of the mall. The ribbon of walkway curved 'round the neat arrangements of scrub pine and mountain laurel, a vain attempt to gentle the harsh bluffs of windowless mallstone.

This path, Jeff thought, this sidewalk where no one walks but me. They built this sidewalk to look like a sidewalk, to make the mall look like a place where humans thrive. In fact, people lock their cars and walk diagonals across the parking lot toward the portals of the mall. No one walks alongside this soulless land-scaping, no one is here but me. Someone once made a model of this mall to impress developers and money men. On that model were these bits of vegetation I'm walking past now. On that model was a little model human. *I* am that model human.

In the synthetic twilight, artifacts glowed amongst the shrubs and shredded cedar bark. A flattened bag of potato chips. A limp piece of curving plastic—insulation left behind from construc-tion. An incongruous chocolate brown rat bait container. Nes-tled in the aromatic green of clipped Japanese yew, a small metal box attached to a stump of pipe. On its side, a red light winked.

"Big Brother is watching." Jeff's grandfather used to say that. When Grampdad was a kid, 1984 was a long way into the future. Now it's ancient history. Here we are, thought Jeff, but we don't know we're here. I know we're here. What good does that do? To know that I'm nothing more than a number? No one has to tor-ture me to get me to behave. No cage of rats around my head. I have no choice but to behave.

Jeff fantasized the Orwellian rats gnawing at his face. If I stand up and die for the cause, what are the chances anyone else will have the courage that I have? So I might as well not fight at all.

But that's what they *want* you to do—give in. They want you to think about the rats and the futility.

I could kick that little box and break it. It would take at least a minute for the security vehicle to find me.

Jeff's peripheral vision told him he was midway between the food court gateway and the Sears gateway. No one had seen him. No one was looking his way.

Jeff tugged open the buttons of his fly and fumbled out his dick. One more glance, right, left. A warm stream drained out of him, downward, onto the device. Soaking it, he used the power of his bladder to violate every crevice. A small piss for man, a giant piss for mankind. Yeah. I'm such a revolutionary. Jeff shook his dick and stuffed it away. I give a shit, that's something. In a few quick strides, he was in the mall.

3

She looked at me. Wait. There. She checked me out again. Danny gazed into the young woman's mascaraed eyes. Like a shy three-year-old, she turned away, faking a peek into the RadioShack window. Danny waited, she did not look back. Come on. Look at me. You know you want to.

If I walked up to her and said something, she'd understand I was picking her up. There's a hotel across the road from this mall, we could be in there in minutes, screwing our brains out. But she probably wouldn't go for that. It isn't like she's licking her lips. She only looked at me for a split second. Maybe her boyfriend is around here someplace. Or maybe she's playing hard to get. Maybe I should be more aggressive. I could do that.

Danny had never picked up a stranger in his life. He was getting older, so if he didn't do it soon he'd never do it. After thirty-seven there isn't a lot to look forward to other than retirement and death. He looked around. Does she think I'm just one more schmo in the mall, wasting time? No, she couldn't think that. Look at me.

She knows I am so much better than this. She knows I'm only here because I have to be here. Look at the way I'm dressed. There isn't one guy up here besides me in a suit. I could drive into the city and get Mom something from Hermès or even Valentino. I can afford it. Believe me, I can. But Mom likes this stuff. I have to shop at the mall like the rest of the cretins. Stand in line with my credit card and deal with the rude salespeople so I can nab some synthetic rag or gold-plated junk. I don't want to be here.

Danny stole another glance at the woman, but she was gone. Danny shot his cuffs and touched his Rolex. So what, I don't care. Waste of time.

Danny's world was a world of perfectly appointed goods and services: Egyptian cotton dress shirts, horsehide shoes made to order, obsequious assistants, manicured fingernails and a flat belly. He chose his cologne with care. His tie pattern was au courant. To relax, he meditated on his retirement accounts. He was in great shape in every way: physically and economically. Of course, he knew there were a few levels perched above him on the ladder of life, but not many. Not many at all. Danny was a player, a genuine individual. He was the kind of person all these slobs wanted to be.

Danny had become a financial consultant six years ago. He was a winner in millennial Lotto. He made money and he traveled all the time. He especially liked the prerogatives of first-class flight—an upgraded seat, a glass of Johnnie Walker Black on the rocks, the little china dish of warmed mixed nuts and a moist hot towel.

Stewardesses liked Danny. They looked him in the eye when they took his drink order. As each forkful of caviar and lobster claw salad was laid upon his plate, they paused, inviting him to strike up a conversation. He'd make a lame joke and they'd laugh at it, hip to his irony. He was what they wanted: young, virile, sharp, with money and a great sense of himself. His banded finger did not repel them. They understood: the kind of man they dreamed about, the kind who married. Compared to the paunchy chardonnay-sucking oldies in the seats around him, Danny was practically James Bond.

And when he deplaned, there was always a graying guy in a uniform clutching a signboard scribbled with Danny's name. He loved the sound the trunk of the shiny black car made as it popped open, the driver deftly storing away his Tumi bags.

Danny figured if he really wanted to, he could invite one of these pretty stewardesses for a lift in his shiny black car. They'd take him up on it. Have a drink with him in the hotel bar. By 11:15 he would be doing the deed and by 11:45 he would be taking a steaming shower, satisfied and fulfilled. He could do that. He could. He just never did.

Danny and his wife, Judy, used to have a great sex life. Then Judy missed her period. After about three months of pregnancy, the sex became more and more sedate. By the eighth month they weren't having sex at all. After Judy gave birth, forget it. At first, she couldn't, because of the pain. Then with 2:00 A.M. feedings, endless baby baths and socializing play dates, the bone-numbing fatigue set in. They started to have sex, at least once a month, and then Judy got pregnant with Timmy. The cycle began again, only worse. Something changed in Judy. She became contented in a way that no longer required sex. Or Danny.

A year ago Danny felt a shooting pain in his groin. He made an appointment with his physician. In the waiting room of the medical center, he flipped through a month-old copy of *Business Week*. He glanced around the room at the fellow sufferers. One sallow, dark-haired woman with a Band-Aid on her nose, one wheezing old man and a pert forty-something bottle blonde. The blonde met his eyes. Danny was girding himself to return the look when he heard his name: "Mr. Marks?"

Within minutes, Danny's pants were around his ankles and the drowsy doctor, Dr. Hershcombe, was massaging his balls. Hershcombe squeezed a testicle. "Does this hurt?" A hatpin of pain pierced Danny's guts.

"Uh—sort of."

"Well, it doesn't look like anything malignant. You do have some swelling."

Danny wondered if the doctor was a homosexual. Would a man be willing to endure the rigors of medical training just to squeeze another man's sack?

"Lie on your side please."

Danny lay on the crinkly white paper and within moments Dr. Hershcombe's latex-armored finger was exploring the nether end of his digestive tract. The pain danced like lightning in a black summer sky. Danny glanced down and saw that not only did he have an erection, but a droplet of cum shone at its tip.

In his office, Hershcombe briskly explained that what Danny was suffering from was, for lack of a better word, blue balls.

"Blue balls?"

"You know, you're all backed up down there. How's sex with your wife?"

"Good. Great. But, not much since, you know—kids."

"Uh-huh." Hershcombe nodded as if he were listening to the confessions of a pederast or serial rapist. As if there were something perverse about Danny's lack of intimacy with his wife. "And how often do you masturbate?"

"I don't masturbate."

"Well, I recommend you do. Or take a mistress. Otherwise, this condition can lead to prostate inflammation and those can be very resistant to treatment with antibiotics."

"You want me to jerk off?"

"To relieve the pressure, yes. Until you can resume regular relations with your wife or until your metabolism slows down and your body stops producing so much semen."

"When will that be?"

"You're thirty-seven? Oh, you'll see a distinct drop-off in the next ten or so years."

Danny walked out past reception. He could feel the sexy nurse checking him out, but couldn't meet her eyes.

As Danny hit the fresh air outside the doctor's office, he felt an intense fatigue. Before today, every doctor's examination had ended with congratulations on his terrific health, good genes, great bones and youthful vigor. He'd been treated for strep a couple of times and, when he was a teenager, had broken a small bone in his foot. Those were simply the hazards of living. This was not about that. Endings were being discussed. "A distinct drop-off" was being discussed.

Even when it was a pain in the ass, sex was always there, it was his friend. It was a persistent reminder of his own lifespring, an atomic engine burning away inside, hooking him up to the powers of the universe. There were times when Danny wanted to fuck everyone. But Danny was happy with Judy and through Judy he had touched the larger spheres of life. They had shared small smiles in the darkness because things were so good for them. They had shared the awesome miracle of having children. As his friend Warren had said, it's like being inside yourself and outside yourself at the same time.

Of course, Warren could talk. He had split up with his wife three years ago and only saw his children every other weekend. Now Warren bedded every female paralegal in his office building. And he seemed very happy. But Danny wasn't Warren. Danny liked a home life. He loved coming home a little late and tiptoeing in and out of the children's rooms, watching them sleep, entering his own bedroom, silently shrugging off his clothing until Judy muffled a plaintive "Honey, is that you?"

Danny loved all that. Except that Danny's balls needed more and had turned blue. In a few more decades Danny's balls would be as dry as two raisins, never mind blue.

Danny hadn't jerked off since college, when he kept a stash of stroke mags hidden under his bed. He was mortified to remember the titles: *Leg Show, Swank, Club, Hustler.* Almost nightly he would fall into long whack-off sessions with the heavy-breasted babes on the glossy pages. Breasts and vaginas came in many, many varieties. The mags Danny would grab up at the bus station were almost clinical in their scrutiny of feminine anatomy. It was an education of sorts, since Danny had never had a chance to really examine any of the girls he "dated."

He wondered if he was the only man who got turned on this way. He couldn't be the only one, since the photo layouts specifically emphasized the gynecological aspects of the models. As he was cumming, it felt terrific to be immersed in images of femininity. He was the center of his own bachelor party. Everyone was delighted to be his sexy plaything. As soon as he came, he'd feel a letdown. Exhausted, he'd see the girls in the photos as tawdry. He'd feel sorry for them. He would see himself, perhaps the whole human enterprise, as ridiculous.

When he started having sex with Judy, her oval breasts and long legs compared favorably to anything he had seen in magazines. Danny had always been proud of that. Judy taught him about passion and lovemaking and making it fresh each time. Soon he grew bored with the simplicity of masturbation. It was repetitive and dumb compared to what he had with his wife-to-be. For Danny it had been a victory to throw away the dirty magazines when he moved in with Judy.

But Hershcombe had ordered him to whack off, it was a medical necessity. And this wasn't the kind of thing he could talk about with Judy. The *Penthouse* and *Hustler* stroke mags didn't do it for him anymore—those photos were for people who never had sex. He tried videos and soon he was in deeper dick-wilting water. The insipid music and grunting actors only reminded him of the kind of trailer trash he saw walking around the mall, the last people on earth he wanted in his fantasies.

One day as Danny was sorting through the mail, glancing at the handful of catalogs that, along with offers of platinum credit cards, came daily, he chanced upon one for silk thermal underwear. Flipping the pages, he found the pictures oddly charming. The photos were so obviously posed, the expressions of the girls so natural. A glimmer of humanity, of true nakedness, revealed itself. Danny felt a thickening, a gentle wooziness. A glow.

Sliding the catalog between the pages of a week-old copy of *Barron's,* Danny withdrew to his cinnamon-scented master bathroom. While Judy made tuna salad on whole wheat and the kids watched a tape of *A Bug's Life,* Danny fantasized loving an anonymous underwear model. These pictures didn't work like the stroke mags of yore, creating hard-edged horniness in his belly. Rather he felt a warm emotion toward the happy young things. The unspoken statement every picture made was "This is what you'll look like to him as you undress, just before you make love." The pictures reminded him of things he used to feel a long time ago.

Soon Danny was inspecting every Sunday department store insert, every catalog and every flyer for delectable morsels of twenty-something flesh. He noticed that different companies had different policies regarding semiclad young women in their flyers. Wal-Mart never featured suggestive pics. Sears sometimes did.

Danny had his favorites, girls who appeared in the Sunday supplement one week, in a woman's magazine the next. He would fantasize being the prim photographer while they, unfettered by any modesty, danced around him in their lacy little panties, laughing and carefree.

It was like he knew them personally, and when they popped up unexpectedly in, say, an L.L. Bean catalog, Danny would greet them like old friends. He wondered what their lives were like, whether they were recognizable for what they did. Did people stop them for autographs? He would.

Danny stood before the Victoria's Secret catalog store staring at the large cardboard-backed photos of models in the window. God. I've become a pervert, he thought. I'm standing here ogling pictures of girls in their underwear. Another voice within him, his devil voice, said, That's right, Danny. That's just what you're doing. Later, when you get home, you're going to lock yourself in the study and pull out that JCPenney catalog and a tube of Judy's Origins hand lotion and you're going to polish the little soldier's helmet till he pukes. It's going to feel great. And then you're going to do it again. Danny couldn't stop his thoughts. His mind had a mind of its own.

Danny imagined himself in his special place, his "study," a custom-built room of wood and leather and tightly packed bookshelves. A place to be alone and get work done. What a joke. For the past six months the only work he'd done in that room was fine-tuning his stroke. He'd be there soon. Alone with his slim, tight-butted, B-cup twenty-two-year-old, the one with the sky blue eyes and surprisingly unfettered sex drive.

Danny tried not to remember the bad parts, when he would have to get down on his hands and knees and carefully wipe the teaspoonfuls of cum off the shiny polyurethaned floor, off the sides of his mahogany desk. Off his horsehide shoes. All he could think was, What an asshole. Because that's what he was. Even though it was doctor's orders.

He had read a magazine article once about "sex addicts." Maybe he was one of those. Maybe he should go to a meeting and sit around with a bunch of twisted freaks and "dialogue" about how he wanted to hold his own private underwear model photo sessions. Yeah, right. A shiver yanked him back to the mall.

Danny blinked and the flow of shoppers surrounding him reappeared. Did anyone notice? No. They were too stupid. This was his world, private and sealed. It was no one's business but his own. He had it all, so what if he had a quirk? That's all it was, a quirk. Time to buy something for Mom and get on home. He had things to do.

4

A bead of sweat traced the small of Mal's spine as he thumped his mother's floppy corpse down the cellar stairs. Past his barbells and bench, past the cartons of *National Geographics*, Mal wrestled it into the shadows behind the oil burner. With industrious care, he piled bundles of newspaper and magazines on top of her soft shape. Her head was the last thing to be covered. A piece of her scalp had been torn off her brow by the second round, an angry red flap that would never heal. Mal dropped the last bundle on it.

With a fastidiousness he had never shown when Mary was alive, Mal soaked the bundles with kerosene, making sure to cover the walls and the dusty playroom floor. He soaked the smelly, mildewed couch pushed up against a flaking wall. He soaked the glassy-eyed mice in their pinewood and copper wire spring traps. He soaked the stairs, working his way back up to the kitchen door, leaving it ajar.

A few minutes later, Mal found himself leaning forward, arms propped straight out before him, facing a surface. He brought his head down until it hung only inches from the fish stick—crumb-covered, cigarette-scarred kitchen thing. What was it? This thing? What did you call it? More and more often Mal was forgetting words. Simple words. Like this thing. *Kitchen tabletop.* Was that it? Didn't sound right. *Kitchen surface.* Fuck it.

On his hand Mal saw a blot and then on his sleeve, a scuff of red. Blood. His? Oh yeah, no. His mom's. *Counter.* That's what it's called. A kitchen counter. For counting? Is that right?

Like a rough asteroid on a wide ellipse around the sun, no matter how far Mal's thoughts strayed from the matter at hand, all things ultimately were drawn by one monstrous gravitational pull. The fish sticks, his mom's cooling body in the basement, even his big scheme were only planets revolving about a massive white-hot star—an appetite for methamphetamine sulfate.

Mal was spent. His eyelids were heavy, dragging him down with thick iron chains to unwanted sleep. He was as lively as a thousand-year-old Galápagos turtle on downs. But in a few moments, because he was a good altar boy–type speed freak, he'd be reborn. To the brink he held off. Did not unwrap the last bits of tinfoil. No. Did not snort the white powder. No. Because he knew in his core, in his eager soul, past his drug-hungry lizard brain, knew that if he waited as long as possible the last hit would be a good hit. He would feel God.

When he finally gave in, he did. The searing lines, stepped on with something nasty and harsh, sliced into his sinuses, then into his brain, and it was not long before all the pistons were firing. Oh, God, no. Thank you, God. Thank you, God, for making my brain and the speed to hook it up with! Yes. The powers will return and everything will be easy again.

The methamphetamine rang up and down Mal's spine like mallets on a xylophone, the hairs stood stiff on the back of his pimply neck, his dick shrunk and his balls drew up inside his undernourished, stringy carcass. Mal was ready for anything. The run had gone on for three days now. And tonight was the night. Tonight Mal would sort things out and finally be able to rest.

Mal reached into his mouth and wiggled a loose tooth. It broke off, its wet red stump contrasting sharply against the yellow enamel. Mal smiled and tossed the tooth back where it came from and swallowed.

5

Donna came up for air. Wow. What just happened? She didn't want to look. The spoon was still in her hand. Splashes of brown stuff streaked her blouse. She forced herself to look. Yup. All gone. Like a magic trick. A half gallon of Winchell's Supreme Rocky Road. Where did it go? Well, it wasn't the *whole* container of ice cream. The guys had some for dessert the night before. Yeah, like five tablespoons.

Donna stood, slightly tipsy. That's a lot of ice cream. Weirdly, she couldn't feel it inside of her. She pinched the container by a soggy edge. It slipped from her fingers onto the faux-parquet linoleum. Yech. I'll clean it later. I need a cigarette. Even though I promised Roy I'd quit. I did quit. Last night. But right now I need a cigarette to get through.

Donna plodded down to the split-level garage. Here the trash barrels lived in twilight beside the snow shovels and old cans of paint. She bent into the container along the wall and rummaged. The butts were down there, in the darkness at the bottom. She knew they were there, she could smell them. Tobacco, come to me.

Donna couldn't see them but she could feel them between her fingers. Past a banana peel. Soggy Kleenex. Coffee grounds. Four or five butts were all she needed. Bottoms of trash cans were always a bit damp. But that was no problem, she knew what to do.

Donna lost her balance for a second and started to tip into the maw of the barrel, catching herself but not before her stomach squeezed hard against the rubbery rim. Oh man, I don't want to puke. Or maybe I do. Stomach acid blended with the cold sugary cream and gurgled up her esophagus. She clenched her throat. She gripped the fistful of damp butts in her hand. Donna was no quitter.

On her way back up to the kitchen, Donna noticed the dust-balls on the steps. Didn't Roy Jr. sweep this week? She dumped the butts into the microwave, set it for thirty and watched the little demons spin in their special light. Thirty seconds is a long time. She had already knocked off half the Oreos. Why not a few more?

The alarm bell of the microwave caught Donna in a food blackout with three Oreos in her mouth. She swallowed the cookie paste, retrieved the butts and finding papers in Roy's stash rolled one good cancer stick.

She would save it. The Oreos had momentarily staved off a complete crash. A purifying hot shower first, then the cigarette, a short drink and all would be well in the world.

Donna surveyed her body in the bathroom's full-length mirror. She was still fine. No matter how much she ate, no matter what she did, she was a robust fox. She could even pose for dirty pictures she looked so good. Which was a wonderful thing except it was all wasted on Roy. Because Roy was clueless on every count. He still turned heads, but he was for shit in bed. What was worse, he thought he was hot stuff.

Donna ran her hand over her belly. Scratched her bush. Scratched her butt. What a waste. She cranked the shower as hot as she could stand and stepped into the steam. As her bellyflesh reddened, Donna realized she was still hungry.

6

Mal inspected his arsenal, booty from road trips to Florida. Mary never suspected he had strayed outside city limits. He'd say he was staying at a girlfriend's place and then pop a couple of black beauties and drive all night. End up just south of Orlando where an old dealer buddy with smudgy blue-green tattoos ran an alligator farm. There was no problem getting everything he needed.

Which wasn't a lot. A man can only carry so much. A Colt Combat Elite .38 loaded with hollow points and a Smith & Wesson Model 17 revolver with a hard rubber grip (.22 caliber for accuracy and reliability). Oh, and the little automatic that took care of his mother, still warm in his pocket. Two Remington auto shotguns, loaded and ready, a Heckler & Koch MP-5 9mm submachine gun and a standard-issue infantry M-16 he picked up at a gun show, just for luck.

Mal felt a chemical wave ripple through his system. His organism—kidneys, heart, lungs, liver, brain, glands—was chugging more at weasel than human speed. He could feel the walls shimmering, the wallpaper floating. The heat of the tiny bedroom closed in, tipping Mal forward onto the bed. He caught his balance before he hit the cold black hardware of his mini-armory.

A long swig from a soft plastic one-liter bottle of Dr Pepper and the molecules within Mal rearranged. The waves of dizziness disappeared. He was left brilliant, shining like the stainless-steel barrel of his .38.

His hands barely shaking, Mal picked a holster off the bedspread and looped it over one shoulder, then mirrored the action so that one nylon and velcro pocket hung under each armpit. One for the .38, one for the .22. He checked the loaded shotguns. Six shells each. Finally he checked the mags of the submachine guns, tapping each on end, then pressing the one visible brass and lead round, testing for springiness. Everything was clean, oiled and rubbed down.

Criss-crossed in his holsters, Mal cradled the shotguns and subguns like cordwood and toted them to his mother's car sitting alongside the house in the carport. A minor debate broke out in his head about the caution he should be taking. His higher consciousness prevailed and told him no one gave a shit what he did. If someone saw him dumping weapons into the trunk of his mother's car, by the time they picked up the phone, he'd be long gone.

Mal returned to the house, now redolent of kerosene. He pulled a baseball jacket over the holstered guns, returned to the bedroom, finished the Dr Pepper and grabbed a gym bag imprinted with the words I Ate the Whole Thing. He dropped in the boxes of shells for the .22 and the shotguns, clips for the .38 and ten banana clips for each subgun. Each item was marked with orange, pink and yellow Day-Glo tape. He didn't want to get confused when it came time to reload.

Mal relished the weight of the machined metal hanging along his flinty ribs. He envisioned the men who fell amongst the sharp gray rocks at Big Top and Little Top, chopped by lead just like the lead he carried. The men at Normandy and Gallipoli, the men of Ia Drang and Pork Chop Hill, the cowboys, the Indians, the Arabs, the Japs and the Nazis, all savaged by metal exploding out of rifled bores. He saw the pale bodies lying still, the salt water or snow or dirt poisoning their punctured flesh.

He fondly reflected on the dozens of rounds and their pinches of gunpowder, each an explosion waiting for a spark. People had no fucking idea what a bullet was. They go to the movies and watch actors shoot hundreds of rounds at each other. They see police proudly display oaktagged weapons piled high on evidence tables. They cluck over front-page photos of thin men raising AK-47s over their turbaned heads. They buy rap records embellished with posed "gangstas" flashing chrome-clad automatics.

Most people never touched a trigger in their lives. Never felt the punch of recoil in their shoulder or palm. Never smelled the perfume of gun oil, the tang of freshly burnt gunpowder. Most wouldn't even know what a safety was if you shoved it up their ass. But they all paid the taxes that bought more machine guns and chain guns and grappling guns. They signed the paychecks of the men who did carry and load and fire those weapons—the cops and the servicemen and the guards—the uniformed bodies who stood between civilization and the ever-rising tide of a hungry, desperate world.

In the blink of an eye a pistol or rifle slung spinning hot metal, breaking bones, severing nerves, slicing arteries, popping vitals. People thought when you shot someone he died but that wasn't necessarily true. You can chop up a body pretty good without killing it. Mal recalled the trainer of gladiators daubing Spartacus's oiled body with paint: "This is a wound. This is a kill."

In the bathroom Mal checked himself in the mirror one last time. His skin swarmed under the fluorescent light. He filled the old Flintstones jelly jar glass with the copper-tasting tap water and swallowed two more black beauties. Patted his pocket for the wad of cash.

In the middle of the aging living room Mal stood still. He could hear his breathing, hear his heart racing. He felt tired, he felt like he should sleep. The plan was moving forward: the dogs were dead, his mother was dead, the gym bag and the guns were in the car. Hit one domino and they all fall down.

Mal trudged into the kitchen. He dug a cloudy bottle of corn oil out of the fridge. Topping off a Revere Ware frying pan with the golden syrup, he set it on the stove and turned up the flame so the blue tips turned yellow. He wadded some paper towels into the crack between the stove and the countertop.

Mal watched the oil pop and sizzle, transfixed. As he did, the talons of the black beauties dug into the back of his head. His skin contracted. Like a field of flowers blooming in one of those speeded-up films on educational TV, the whole room exploded into confetti-colored geometric patterns. Mal looked around slack-jawed. Here I am. I am everything. Everything is me. I move. Everything moves.

A burp of hot oil splashed onto the paper towels. Blue flame trickled to the tinder and it blushed brown, then red, then curled wickedly into itself.

Mal watched with a deep contentment. Fire fixes everything.

He smiled, the gaps in his mouth as vivid as his yellow teeth. He laughed like a little boy, but the sound he made was a hoarse, coughing bark.

7

Jeff wandered the cave of the mall. Vague music played somewhere. Sounds of children, someone talking close by. The murmur of material desire filled the space.

Like a refugee on a forced march Jeff moved with the crowd. Everyone wants to be an individual. Everyone wants to wear special things and cut their hair in special ways and learn special lingo, so that they can be an individual. But there are too many slots to fill. The more individual everyone tries to be, the more alike they all are. Did I read that somewhere?

And I'm like them in almost every way. Why don't I just admit it? I'm just a suburban boy propelled from nothing to nothing. But I'm also not. Deep down, I know that. From the outside, no one knows what I have inside, but that's my secret. It's a secret I have to keep. Because they don't care anyway.

Jeff's secret was that he knew he was a genius. He could feel it in his bones. Someday he would be a famous writer. He would pile words into vast mansions of thought and expression and the world would look up at them with admiration and amazement.

Jeff didn't get the highest grades in school, but that was because he knew grades were only a measure of spineless conformity. And fuck college. He didn't have one hero who had a B.A., so who needed that shit? He'd get around to mastering style and coherence. Those things came with time. Technique was just a matter of practice. The important thing was insight and the wisdom you get from living life. That was what Jeff wanted to focus on. Living and loving and experiencing everything he could find. Make every second count.

Jeff dropped in on the CVS store and wandered around, checking out foot powders and eyewash and high-potency vitamins. He floated by the cash register, picked up a Bounty candy bar and a pack of gum, then put them back. Stealing was a science.

Jeff ambled toward the back of the store. An Asian woman waited patiently for her prescription while the old pharmacist dicked around. Jeff picked up an Ace bandage and a large bag of sterile cotton balls. On his way back to the front, he grabbed a rollerball pen and a small pad. He waited in line with the Ace bandage and the cotton balls, then patting his pockets like he'd forgotten his wallet, left the stuff behind and walked out of the store with the pen and the pad in his pocket.

There was no moral issue here, nothing to be debated. He needed a pen and some paper and they were there to be taken. He'd never been caught because no one who worked at the store could be bothered watching him pick things up and put them down and go through the whole charade. Fluorescent light destroyed the will in people.

Jeff stepped out of the store and back into the flow of the

mall. Two small boys in classic Gap togs tore past. One tripped and skidded sideways, slamming his face flush into a rectangular brick planter in the middle of the polished floor. The kid was stunned, but said nothing. The blood trickled out of his nose and his brother started screaming.

Before Jeff could cover the few steps toward the children, a large parental male in a baseball cap grabbed the bleeding boy by the wrist and tugged him up sharply, at the same time glowering at Jeff's raggedy hair.

"Did I tell you no running? Did I? Now look what happened. You got blood all over your new sweatshirt. Come on, your mother's gonna kill both of us."

Jeff added this to his inventory of observations. Maybe he could start a chapter with it. It said so much about materialism. Said so much about the spiritual desert we occupy. And blood was always a good symbol. What was it a symbol of? Blood. Blood was a symbol of blood? He'd have to do it in an ironic way. Maybe the father has a heart attack as he's dragging the kids away.

Jeff was always trying to collect catalysts for writing ideas. He'd take long walks in the woods. Once, he discovered an area where there had been a quarry. Equipment had been left there, abandoned, rusting. Scattered amongst the ruins of cranes and conveyor belts and wheel-less bald tires were barrels leaking something tan and sudsy.

Jeff had read about a reservoir near a gold mine that had burst and poisoned a nearby river, killing all the fish and birds and frogs. In Africa and Asia civil war and landmines had cleared vast stretches of acreage, unsuitable for farming ever again. In the tropics, mangrove swamps and coral reefs died by the tens of acres every day. It was only a matter of time before the boundaries of the ever-widening toxic killing fields intersected, and then the world would be nothing more than a big ball of dead dirt.

Jeff had grown up harangued by elementary school teachers and educational television, forced to participate in endless "ecology awareness days" and "special projects," all to alleviate the endless evils created by mankind. To know rain forests were burning into extinction was a cliché. It was as if a fire were raging on the horizon and everybody knew that sooner or later it would get to where they were standing. Like that story in Laura Ingalls Wilder's *Little House on the Prairie.*

And sometimes it seemed the only person who saw the fire was Jeff. He understood that where he lived was not human. Computers and corporations had joined forces to make his world. Scented candle shops, lingerie shops, hot cookie shops, Disney shops—inhuman crap for the masses. The massive machine-driven bureaucracies knew what people liked. They polled and sorted human desire and they delivered.

Didn't anyone else see how scary this was? How it left no room to move? What did it mean to be human anyway? Just to procreate and walk around and buy lawn ornaments?

Jeff had read all the dystopian novels: *Brave New World, 1984, A Clockwork Orange, The Handmaid's Tale;* everything by William Gibson. But they were all set in the future. That was a lie. The future was here, now.

Last week Jeff, Terry and Beckett had borrowed Beckett's parents' car and gone to a nightclub in the city. It wasn't really a nightclub, but an old high-ceilinged factory space, all painted in matte black. At one end stood a bandstand, at the other a soft drink and juice bar. No liquor. The braying skinhead bands rose up one after another, indistinguishable. A skinny girl with a ring in her nose slouched beside a green-haired "goth." Jeff wondered what he had in common with them.

Each band featured a guitar player, a drummer and a tattooed guy sporting a shaved pate who screamed into a mic. Each steroidal band played, thrashed around the stage and thumped into the shirtless young men who clambered up to mix with their leaders. Every few minutes someone dove off into the throbbing crowd. Jeff liked the extra-loud grinding music. It hooked his gut in a satisfying way. He noted the singer in one band had swastikas tattooed on both arms.

Everyone around him was howling. Although the place had no license to serve booze, every kid was drunk on beer or wasted on Special K. The fun lay in getting up close to the stage and churning into the mosh crowd. Particularly aggressive guys would thrust out as if picking a fight, eyes down like belligerent mental patients. Jeff knew the rules—don't shove back too hard unless you wanted to get hit even harder.

Occasionally one of the aggressive shovers would push another aggressive shover and the punching would start. Then the very large and even more muscular bouncers would jump in and warn the fighters. Eventually someone would get thrown out of the club. Jeff saw one guy with a bloody nose. Everyone knew the rules, no knives, no face stomping or rib kicking. They were well-behaved anarchists.

Bodies tumbled into bodies, as if the floor had tilted off-balance. It was exhausting and, in the end, good. The rage, the noise and the bloody teeth were therapy for testosterone overdose. By the end of the night, the big black box of a room stunk like a sweat-soaked jockstrap.

Terry, loopily drunk, let Beckett and Jeff drop him home so he could throw up. The two survivors smoked a joint while swinging on Terry's rusty backyard swingset. They tramped the vacant streets till 3:30 in the morning and argued about causality in the universe. Beckett called Jeff "superstitious" because he believed in a life force. Jeff didn't have the energy to debate him.

Later, Jeff fumbled through his parents' front door, keys jangling way too loud as they hit the kitchen table. Lights on, lights off. Trying to stay upright in the bathroom, ears ringing, dreads thick with dried sweat, Jeff felt silly. As the bland dawn light softened the scrubbed tiles around him, he meditated on the crumpled toothpaste tube. He tried to imagine how many toothpaste tubes like this one were in the United States, in the world, right now. Did people think about them? They thought about them enough to choose them. To choose this brand. They ever notice how repetitious it all was?

Somewhere, he was sure, were some very rich people who were the inheritors of the wealth that came from selling all this toothpaste. Hopefully those rich people were free in a fundamental way. Really free. Jeff didn't want to be rich. He didn't even care if he was free. He just wanted to believe that someone, somewhere was free. One soul existed outside this grid.

All these things he wanted to talk over with Adelle. She would understand. She was deep and wise. Together they would face the doomed world. It gave Jeff courage to believe he could share this struggle with someone. She would lie in his arms, entwined physically and emotionally. Together they would face whatever was coming.

If he could connect with her it wouldn't be so futile. One person who understood was all he needed. Alone he was like a dot on a piece of paper. A connection to Adelle made a line from his dot to hers. A line creates another dimension altogether.

Jeff sensed his eyes were closed. He moved an arm and a sheet rustled. He was in bed. Had he brushed his teeth? He didn't care. Emptiness was all there was, an unfilled space from something to something, but he couldn't remember what. Adelle. Adelle. Adelle. Love was a hard thing. Would he feel different when he awoke? He wasn't sure. He wasn't sure of anything. The spaces between his thoughts grew, yawned into a chasm, and he plummeted.

8

The streams of red and white draped over the landscape like long ropes of glowing candy. Each pair of headlights a vehicle, identical from afar. Each set of lights an individual, encased in metal and plastic, following a plan. Coursing like blood cells, slipping past one another, never colliding, orderly, speeding into the flattened landscape of the next moment.

Cocooned amid the constructed contours of her car, Donna drove at her usual whipping fifty-in-the-thirty, eighty-in-the-sixty pace. She'd been stopped dozens of times and never gotten a ticket. Not one. She touched the steering wheel lightly as she maneuvered a large Coffee Coolatta drink and what remained of the dozen donuts she had just picked up.

Cruising, feeling spaced after the hot shower and the whiskey, air conditioner on high, she had spotted the donut shop and decided to buy a coffee. Driving and drinking coffee seemed to be the right thing to do. She could drive around for a while, ingest caffeine, sober up, pick up dinner for everybody and be home at a reasonable time. That was the plan as she pulled into the parking lot of the Dunkin' Donuts.

While waiting for the pockmarked Pakistani to fill another order, Donna caught the eye of a trucker hunched over a dinky table. He was penciling in his word puzzle book. The trucker noticed Donna and gave her a deep look that went straight to her groin. She liked it, but forced herself to turn away, only to find herself facing racks and racks of freshly fried donuts. Something about waiting in line made her hungry. One donut wouldn't hurt.

Donna couldn't settle on which donut, they all looked so delectable. She figured she would buy a half dozen and decide later. Eat two and bring the rest home to Roy and Roy Jr. Then she noticed they were having a special on something called a Coffee Coolatta. So she decided to have one of those too. As she trotted out of the shop with her donuts and five-million-calorie drink, she glanced at the trucker. He smiled. She smiled back. Next time.

Back in her vehicle, Donna drove and ate and felt that fine complete sensation of harmony. She was moving, she was eating. Donna pondered her fulfillment as she brought the cinnamon-apple jelly donut to her lips, grabbed a chunk between her white teeth and pulled it onto her tongue. Why couldn't it be like this always? She didn't need heroin. She didn't need crack. She just needed donuts. And a nice fuck. And a cigarette after. And a shot of ice-cold bourbon.

At least she had the drinking under control. She could put that in the plus column. Hadn't wrinkled a fender or blown up a dinner party for over a year. That was the thing she hated most about Roy. (Funny how deeply you could hate the person you loved.) When they first met, Roy got a big kick out of her drinking. He laughed at how uninhibited she was when she was drunk. How sexy she could be. Of course, she had to be ram-bunctious, Roy was such a dead trout.

Now he had drawn borders around acceptable and unaccept-able, watching over her like a prison guard. Fortunately for Donna, Roy did not understand how appetite worked. How it could move from one thing to another. Being drunk was nice, yes. Nothing like a warm bath and a tumbler of gin. But so was food, and so was sex. All were good things.

She wondered if she never stopped eating if she would start getting really fat. For some reason, she wasn't fat yet. She knew she was softer and heavier. Her breasts were big and her butt was full. But she wasn't fat. She had no creases around her middle. She had no cellulite on her thighs. The flesh under her arms was taut. After birthing a kid, her nipples still stood out like baby gumdrops.

It was inevitable she would grow larger. Then if she really got down at the trough, well, like she was eating today, she'd have to get fat. Hell, in the last three hours she had consumed about five or six thousand calories.

Would she just get bigger and bigger? Would she still be pretty? Deep down, Donna didn't care. Somehow she knew it would all work out. It would have to work out. Because her ap-petite was her best friend. Her appetite took care of her and car-ried her through the bad parts. She *was* her appetite, without it there was no Donna.

Maybe she would get huge. Be one of those people who fit snugly in extra-large sweatsuits, all rumpled and lumpy, waddling around covered with crumbs and ice-cream stains. She'd be happy. And she'd just keep eating until she exploded.

9

The bookstore loomed. Jeff entered it, drawing not one curious glance from the clerk at the register. In the clothing stores, if he entered with his dreads and his tattered clothing and his knapsack emblazoned with a skull and crossbones, an assistant manager would be on him before he could get ten feet in the doorway. "May I help you?" As if help were actually being offered. It was a threat which said, "If you're not buying something, get out. I know you're here to steal."

There were no big-ticket items in a bookstore, so everyone was pretty relaxed. The place felt more like a toy store than a library. You had to get past the piles of rubbish up front in order to get to the real books in the back. *South Park* T-shirts and posters, novelties in mesh bags, coffee-table books on gardening or the castles of Scotland, greeting cards, remainders stacked and stickered with large red sale tags, out-of-date semierotic bikini calendars, cute dog calendars, sports calendars, Filofax inserts, pencils and pens, jigsaw puzzles, incense, candles, posters of teen idols. No books. Certainly nothing Charles Dickens or Fyodor Dostoyevsky or Franz Kafka would identify as a book.

Jeff wended his way to the unpopulated back of the store. Very few people went there. He passed the how-to computer books one aisle over, the losing weight books, the New Age ("You are not a human being trying to be spiritual, you are a spiritual being trying to be human"), the business books and finally the children's nook, stocked with bloody horror novelettes by R. L. Stine. For Jeff's peers there was the science fiction section and the mystery section and the romance novels. Jeff passed by these as well. His goal was an area defined by two compact shelves of volumes facing each other, the universe humbly titled "literature."

As small as this section was, a few hundred titles, Jeff could stay here and always find new things. He couldn't afford to buy them, but he could pick up one and read a section. Lately he had been perusing Hesse. He wasn't exactly sure who Hesse was, but he liked the picture on the cover of the Penguin Classics edition. He had a warm feeling for Penguin Classics. Each volume was a gateway to another world.

Jeff glanced up at the front counter, could see that the cashier had forgotten about him. He picked up a book and started reading where he had last left off:

> You have no doubt guessed long since that the conquest of time and the escape from reality, or however else it may be that you choose to describe your longing, means simply the wish to be relieved of your so-called personality.

Jeff dropped down into lotus, pushed his back into the huge cardboard *Beavis and Butt-head* display at the end of the aisle and settled down to read.

10

Mal maneuvered his mother's car with calm precision. He had no need to rush because the ride only took five minutes no matter how tangled the traffic. Carefully using his signal, he turned into the E-Z Gas, parked to one side in the shadows, away from the pumps, popped the trunk and took out five five-gallon cans. Mal passed them to the attendant.

"Fill 'em with high test."

"High test doesn't work good with lawn mowers."

"I'm not mowin' any lawns, chief."

Mal ambled into the twenty-four-hour convenience store that replaced the full-service garage that had stood in that spot for forty years. When Mal was in his teens he had dreamed of being a mechanic there, levitating the Mustangs and Impalas on the hydraulic lifts. He imagined a heaven on earth where he could don overalls every morning, wash down a fistful of white crosses with a sizzling Coke and fiddle with the undersides of GTOs until he was black with grease. The garage and the dour Pall

Mall–smoking mechanics were long gone. Everything good was long gone.

As Mal entered the overlit space of the convenience store, a little plastic box over the door gave off an electronic *ding*. Mal appraised the closed-circuit camera jutting out from the wall. Take my picture, motherfucker, you can run it on the eleven o'clock news! Mal stepped over to the displays of cookies and snacks. A wave of nausea roiled his intestines as he recalled the employment he'd had for two years, rack-jobbing stainless-steel multipronged contraptions of fake food just like these. Wheeling the cardboard cartons in on his hand truck, filling up the empty slots with pink and white and black cake. Lifting and sorting, stacking and carting, chopping up the cardboard. Put my ass into that job and didn't get a thing for it other than a shit paycheck and a permanent ache in my spine.

Mal snatched a cellophane fifty-count pack of Oreos. He stepped over to the wall of refrigerated beverages and grabbed a quart of flavored half-and-half. Making his way back to the register, he waited like a statue with his stuff while the obese bitch behind the counter blabbed on the phone and kept an eagle eye on her skinny customer. She'd had her eye on him from the moment he came through the door. She had watched his hands as Mal moved through the aisles.

". . . I said, 'Tim, I'm not sure I feel right about this.' And he said, 'But I'm tired of her. And I want you and I've been waiting . . .' Oh shit, Cherese? I should get off. There's some freak wants something. Call me back in five minutes."

Once she had hung up the phone, the fat sullen counter girl stopped eyeing Mal and wordlessly addressed his purchases. In fact, she made a point of not looking at him at all. She rang up the stuff and then, finally looking Mal in the eyes, said, "With the gas, fifty-two."

"Pack a Luckies."

She tossed a deck of cigarettes at Mal like a dog biscuit.

"Regulars."

She picked up the cigarettes and replaced them with the smaller pack of unfiltereds. "Fifty-five."

Mal threw two twenties, a ten and a five on the counter and with a frown the girl snapped them up. It was Mal's turn to stare.

"Gonna give me a bag?"

She bagged the items.

"Matches?"

She flipped the folded cardboard square into the bag. As Mal crunched his fist around the top, he paused and looked the girl in the eye.

"You should go on a diet. You're overweight."

"And you smell and you have bad breath."

Mal felt the weight of his guns in their holsters. He smiled his gappy smile.

"You think so?"

"Yeah."

"If you think my breath smells, you should taste my cock after it's been jammed up your chubby pink butt."

The girl froze.

"My sperm would be a lot healthier for you than the shit you've been eating."

She glanced at something behind the counter.

"Would you like that? Would you like to do that? Would you like to suck my shit-covered prick?"

"No."

"Then when somebody gives you advice, be polite enough to take it and say thank you."

"Thank you."

"You wanna push that little red button, go ahead. But be ready for the consequences, 'cause right now all I'm doing is talking. Believe you me, I can do a lot more."

Mal stared at her for a full ten seconds more. Then the little bell chimed and someone came in. Mal reluctantly shifted his weight and moved off. He hadn't felt this good in years.

11

Donna smoothed the blouse down over her breasts, checking out how the mounds pushed through the silky red rayon. She pulled up the lank material and checked out her belly, snuggled the pants down, then her panties, revealing the very top of the curly brown hair down there. She didn't look any fatter than she did this morning.

She was a hot piece of flesh. Yes. She licked her lips at her reflection in the changing room mirror. Maybe some bored security asshole somewhere was watching her on closed-circuit TV. Good. I hope he has a huge hard-on. I hope he's jerking off.

Through the slit in the little curtain covering the door of the changing room, Donna caught movement in the corner of her eye. She froze. Not out of fear, out of curiosity. Someone is watching me. She turned her back to the doorway and tugged her pants off. As she did, she glanced into the mirror once more, finding a new angle through the slit and out into the room. Yes. There's a guy out there. A guy in a suit. Kind of good-looking.

Oh yeah. Pretending to be shopping for stone-washed jeans. He's checking me out.

A bubble of fun expanded in Donna's chest. How far can this go? She toyed with the possibilities. The great thing about a dressing room is that it's a public place where you can go butt-naked and no one can stop you. Donna felt her skin tingle and her nipples get itchy.

As methodically as a stripper, she wriggled out of her jeans, pulled off the red blouse and, clad in nothing more than panties and socks, innocently slid the soft cotton down over her full bum and her smooth knees. She left her socks on, bending over and adjusting each one with care.

He's out there. If he didn't have a boner before, he's got one now. Uh-huh. Check it out, Mr. Businessman. A horny house-wife. I bet you haven't seen anything like this for a long time, if ever. Virtually naked, Donna turned 'round and sat on the tiny changing room bench. She spread her legs wide, as if she were examining a freckle on the inside of her thigh. Then she looked up through the crack in the curtain and smiled a big toothy smile.

12

Michel stood at his usual post, the intersection of the southwest and south wings—two doors down from the McDonald's, four doors from the bank, around the corner from the jewelry store. His legs were throbbing. He stood because he wasn't allowed to sit. The weight of the blood pounded into the capillaries of his feet.

The hard polyester of his uniform pulled tight against his bulk, compressing him further, adding pressure and with that, heat. A fine gloss of sweat stood on his large forehead; even his close-cropped curls were damp against his chestnut skin. Michel did not frown. That would have compromised his commitment to this job. He smiled, barely revealing the gold tooth cap that matched the heavy chain around his wrist.

Michel's extra-large physique had put food on the table since he was a homeless teenager in Port-au-Prince. There was always a use for a fellow like him. Once, when he was only seventeen, he was told to accompany a man in a pink seersucker suit. Michel followed the man to a corner where the local ne'er-do-wells perched on crates, playing dominoes on a scuffed kitchen table.

The man in the pink suit nodded at Michel, raised a pink arm and pointed out a dapper mustachioed man. Michel stepped forward and punched him so hard, the man's jaw cracked on the zinc tabletop as his face dropped to the ground. One punch. The skinny man lay still. Six years later the man in the pink suit was arrested, blindfolded and shot in a prison yard.

When Michel got married to Marie his only desire was to get away from the Ton-Ton Macoutes and the men in the seersucker suits. So he and Marie emigrated. They found work with a corporation supplying night janitors for the high-tech companies slotted into the landscape along the interstate. Michel and his wife would enter the depopulated corridors every night at ten o'clock and, trundling a large wheeled rubbish bin festooned with spray bottles, brushes, toilet paper rolls and flattened dark green plastic trash bags, emptied each cubicle of its crumpled paper and fast-food residue. They vacuumed the industrial-strength rugs and Windexed the plate glass. They refilled the soap dispensers and sanitized the empty toilet stalls.

Michel loved the 2:00 A.M. lunch breaks, sharing cold chicken sandwiches with his quiet Marie and taking the time to smoke a cigarette. Later, riding home in the dank Econoline van with the other immigrant workers, he would say a prayer of thanks to the Madonna. He felt protected.

Toward the end of the second year, Marie had trouble waking up in the morning. She began to cough. She hated the northern winters but had never complained. When she couldn't make it to work for three days in a row, Michel took an afternoon off and brought her to the doctor.

Michel had never seen the inside of a doctor's office before. The smell of disinfectants and the grim people frightened him. Dr. Patel informed them that the cold was not a cold, and that he'd detected a small lump in Marie's chest.

Marie spoke to her mother in Haiti, a devout Catholic who also believed in voodoo. Marie's mother in turn asked the advice of a *mambo*. The priestess took half the monthly money from the States and used it to assemble concoctions and appeal to the *loas,* the saints, on Marie's behalf. She told Marie's mother, who in turn told Michel, that Marie would get better as soon as Michel cut down the papaya tree nearest her window. But no papayas grew where they were. More money was sent. A package containing a hollow gourd, beans and corn and a small bundle of dried leaves arrived in the mail. Michel was to make an infusion of the leaves with bull's bile. He left the magic things untouched on the kitchen table.

It took two months for Marie to wither and die. Every night, Michel dropped heavily to his knees and prayed. He prayed to the Father and Mary. And to be on the safe side he prayed to Ogou Balanjo and Dambala, the serpent spirit and any other spirit he could remember from the dozen or so white wailing voodoo ceremonies he attended as a little boy. He became a child again, frightened again. Whatever was attacking Marie was more horrible than the machetes of the Ton-Ton. Sometimes, he could do no more than hulk over his heavy knees and cry.

Every night Michel sat alone at the kitchen table and filled out the company's insurance forms, or spoke on the phone with impatient resident interns at the hospital. He tried to ignore his boss's irritation over late days and his need for the insurance.

Michel maneuvered Marie's small limp body from specialist to specialist. Once she was locked away in the hospital, he came early every day and waited patiently by the admitting desk to make his visit. She had never had much to say in the first place, so he simply sat and held her hand. Eventually he got permission to stay overnight. He would pull his chair alongside the chromed bars of the hospital bed, resting his heavy head on the sky blue synthetic blanket.

After Marie's funeral, Michel felt hollowed out and refilled with darkness. Things got tense at work, his boss never forgiving him for the lost hours and the use of the insurance coverage. Michel spoke to no one and came home to an empty apartment.

The friendly usurer from whom Michel had borrowed money called and said all would be forgiven if Michel would help him out with a problem. Michel knew what he meant by problem, but didn't care. He would do what he was asked.

Michel was told to meet a man named Chink, who was always chewing gum and who was not Chinese, in the city. Together they walked into a decrepit tavern. Behind the bar was an obese man in his sixties and a younger man in his forties with dark circles under his eyes. The fat man was perched on a bar stool, the younger guy was scratching off Lotto cards one after another.

Michel had been told to remain quietly behind Chink, and so he did. Chink spoke in whispers to the two men. The younger guy kept trying to see around Chink, trying to see Michel in the dark bar light, to size him up. At first the old fat guy glowered and spoke back to Chink, then Chink said a few more words and he grew quiet.

Then the younger man came from around the bar holding a tire iron. He shouted at Michel and swung the black stick.

With a simple sad move, Michel took the iron away from the scrawny barkeep's son, and as Chink watched with dead occidental eyes, Michel slapped the younger man's arm with the steel. Like a dry stick, the bone snapped.

The next day Michel didn't get up off the large rectangle of foam that served as his bed. He asked the Madonna for forgiveness. That night a woman who lived in the next-door flat brought him some soup and he miraculously made it to work the next day. Unfortunately, he had neglected to call in and the boss fired Michel.

Now Michel manned his post as guardian of the mall. His job was to stand there, watching the river of people amble by, swinging their large paper department store bags, pushing strollers, eating ice creams. A living deterrent to petty mall shenanigans.

Michel made a deal with himself. He would become so dependable and so able at what he did that bosses would have no choice but to shower praise upon him. Bosses would be happy to see him. He would be a credit to himself and the memory of Marie. He would pay penance for his sins.

Michel watched the white suburbanites. They seemed happy, but he didn't know much about them. He wasn't even sure how they made a living. They had unemotional faces and endless credit and cash. As he had heard over and over, they were descendants of people who had immigrated just as he had. To succeed like they had was only a matter of industry and thrift.

Every night Michel returned home to his empty flat. He gulped down his fish stew. He sat in a chair. He smoked cigarettes, now lighting one on the end of the last. Sometimes he found himself in his tiny bathroom, looking into his own eyes, wondering, Where was Marie now?

Michel had scraped up the money to send her body to Haiti. Her mother had insisted. He hoped she was still there, that her soul was resting. He knew that souls sometimes had a hard time finding peace and he was sure Marie wanted to be here with him. Michel tried praying, but now every time he got down onto his knees his mind filled with demons and snakes. He welcomed the morning when he could be back at his post.

13

Jeff craned his neck to check the clock behind the cash register. If he was going to hook up with the gang he should get around to it. But something about hanging with them made him feel unclean. When he was alone, he remained pure in his thoughts. When he was with them, he said things he regretted. It was his role in the group to speak too quickly, to say things Beckett could deftly swat and crush.

Last week Jeff made a casual remark about how lame bands are today. He went so far as to champion the folk singers of the early sixties. Beckett was on him like white on rice, ridiculing the whole folk song movement as nothing more than a bunch of white middle-class kids ripping off authentic rural ballads. Jeff couldn't think of an answer to that. He didn't really know much about folk music. When he was around Beckett, he didn't feel like he knew much about anything. But deep down, he knew he did.

Beckett always made the instant impression of self-possession, of having something you wanted. Even if Jeff could give a rat's turd about Beckett's opinion of himself, Jeff knew having confidence like Beckett's ranked high with women, particularly women like Adelle.

Though Adelle and Beckett rarely spoke to each other, Jeff could sense the sexual tension between them. They were afraid of each other and attracted at the same time. Neither would concede to the other's dry power. And Adelle and Beckett and Jeff were, as far as he knew, the only true nonvirgins of the group.

With only one girl had Jeff made a real effort to be a "boyfriend." He called her every night. They went to movies together and talked about them afterward. He even met her parents. They had sex three times. Jeff figured this must be love.

One night she sat patiently at a strip mall diner table while Jeff told her about William Burroughs. He knew she wasn't listening. In a way, he didn't mind. It was still interesting. One of her friends from school came in the door of the diner and in that moment there was nothing more between Jeff and his new girlfriend. Jeff's disinterest created disinterest. What was worse, Jeff didn't care.

Jeff couldn't imagine doing with Adelle what he did with that girl. Of course he knew that should his love be "requited" (as the English teacher put it), sex would be part of it. If and when he had sex with Adelle it would be on a level unlike any he had experienced. Sex had been messy and embarrassing; he could never get past the feeling of being with a stranger. He kissed and groped and tried to touch the things he was meant to touch. The girl would writhe and buck and make sounds but Jeff was pretty sure that whatever she did with him, she did with every guy. Sex with Adelle would be unique, transcendental and full of light.

Jeff needed to talk to Adelle, to spend some time with her and make her laugh. He felt weak behind the knees imagining a simple act like holding her hand or getting close enough to smell her scent. Lying next to her warm smooth body was more than he could imagine.

But Adelle treated Jeff like a person who had no sexual charisma at all, like a bus driver or the school janitor. Maybe that was her way? She was not particularly demonstrative with any of his friends. For the most part she sat and listened to what the others said. Or she smoked cigarettes. It would be a true tragedy if she felt about him the way he felt about her but was so in fear of the power of her emotions that she never dared bridge the gap.

Jeff didn't know how it would happen, but sooner or later, he would spend time alone with Adelle. They would talk and her green eyes would light up with the recognition that a genuine and feeling person was entering her life.

Jeff couldn't stay in the bookstore forever. But the thought of finding the gang and in turn seeing Adelle made his stomach flutter. He stood, shaking the pins and needles from his legs. The store was empty, the manager pulling the glass doors shut at the front. Jeff walked briskly toward the diminishing slot. He considered acknowledging the manager, nodding or saying "Hi," but then discarded the idea. Jeff was the invisible existential man, the loner who frequents bookstores and acts strangely. His very presence called the manager's whole life into question. There was no need for more than that between them.

"You buying that?"

The manager was looking at Jeff's hand, which still held the copy of *Steppenwolf.*

"Uh, yeah . . ."

"Just a minute."

Instead of slipping out into the mall flow, Jeff was sucked back in, forced to perform the ritual of standing patiently while the manager wheezed around the counter, got out his keys and turned the cash register on again.

How old was this guy? Forty? Fifty? Why was he here, doing this job, in a mall? How does that happen? The man was wearing a white shirt, plain black pants cinched tightly around his thick middle. Jeff's mind roamed over his idea of the man's life: the Taco Bell meal digesting in his belly, the TV show he'd watch when he got home, the heart attack he was sure to have in a year or two. The man had given up. His life meant nothing and he knew it.

Maybe the man liked to read and was willing to work in a crappy mall job just to be near his beloved books. Maybe he was a tragic Kafka-esque writer, living an outwardly normal life while dissecting his soul in his private moments. Jeff scrutinized the puffy flesh under the eyes, under the throat. Age, a tragic thing. The washed-out blue eyes, the pinkness of his nosebulb gave no sign of intellectual life. This man was nothing more than a shape occupying space.

"Twelve ninety-five with tax, thirteen ninety-nine." Fourteen dollars. Too much. Not that Jeff didn't have it, but if he was going to hang with the gang later, he had to have at least enough to buy french fries.

"Uh. Never mind. Thanks."

Jeff loped out of the store. He imagined the manager retiring to the minuscule office in the back to count the night's receipts and perhaps return to his bookmarked Stephen King. Then, as Jeff reentered the hall of the mall, he forgot the manager altogether and any empathy he had for him. The bookstore clerk faded then melded into the vast chorus of nobodies who populated Jeff's unhappy globe.

14

This was getting interesting. How long could it go on? Donna slid her panties on leaving her top bare, took her panties off again. Every few seconds she would peek out. Yup, the guy was still out there. Watching. His hard-on must be a mile long. Donna was getting hot, showing every square inch of her fine bod to this stranger only a few feet away. Using ingenuity she managed to bend over, stretch, twist and spread herself in such a way that this guy was getting to know her as well as Roy did.

Danny was numbly suspended in a viscous jelly of excitement. He almost felt nauseous. The last time he checked no salespeople or cashiers or guards were in the vicinity. Danny had inched from the stone-washed jeans to a table of bright cotton tees outside the dressing room. Three giant steps and he could touch her.

Danny could feel his heart through his shirt, his breath coming shallower. She couldn't be more than thirty. This was no posed photograph in a catalog, this was a real girl, a beautiful real

girl, stripping and posing for him in her panties. What should
he do?

Should he say something to her? Should he jump into the
dressing room? Whip out his cock? Then what? Vague black
shapes took form along the horizon of Danny's consciousness.
Perhaps there were sharp rocks in these happy warm seas? Perhaps this situation was a problem, not a solution. Danny ignored
the black shapes. He took one step closer, no longer faking
glances at bar-coded price tags but simply standing, staring into
the slit of the dressing room curtain.

Behind the wall of dressing rooms lay a corridor of blank wall-
board, taped and spackled but left unpainted. Behind this wall
was a suite of windowless rooms. A room for smoking, a pair of
employee bathrooms and a room filled with black-and-white
video monitors.

In this room, disregarding regulations, the female security officer had called the male security officer over to one particularly interesting screen. "What the hell is she doing?" "Is she doing that
for us?" "Either that or she has a great fantasy life." "Look, look
there, she's looking outside, she's aiming herself, she's *posing!*"

When Danny felt the tap on his shoulder it was like he had lost
his balance and fallen backward into the deepest hole ever dug.
Before he could turn around, he knew his life was ruined. If he slit
his wrists, life couldn't have flowed out of him faster. The best
solution was to ignore the tap on his shoulder, and stare even
more intently at the now empty gap in the dressing room curtain.

"Sir."

The tap was hard and firm, a cop's tap. Danny felt himself being turned to face what at first appeared to be a dissociated
clump of floating yellow meat. All the information was there,
blue clothing, badge, bits of brass, eyes, nose. Danny, who had

been concentrating so hard on nicer things like nipples and knees and ribs, could not now focus on the ugly and mundane everyday world.

"Sir, please explain to me what you are doing?"

"I'm shopping."

"What are you shopping for?"

Out of the corner of his eye, Danny could see a matronly security guard ushering the woman, now fully clothed, out of the dressing room. Another security guard came up alongside the cop.

"He was standing there watching her and playing with himself."

The cop took in the info, keeping his eyes on Danny.

"Sir, you'll have to come with me."

"What did I do?"

"Just follow me, sir. Thanks, Al, you don't have to wait around. I saw him. We'll take care of it from here. Get a report from you tomorrow."

Al fidgeted. This wasn't enough. "What about the young lady?"

"There's no law against taking your clothes off in a dressing room, Al."

"But she was posing for him."

"Yeah, well, she's got a bright future."

Like a funeral usher, the cop took Danny by the elbow. Solemnly they moved past the racks of young ladies' wear and toward the side entrance leading out to the parking lot. Danny could see another cop, this one chatting into a two-way radio, standing by the glass doors.

Danny was crisply in the moment now. Everything clearly outlined, colors bright, almost pulsing. As he walked, flanked by the cop, he imagined how this was going to go. They were going to charge him with something. Worse, they would phone his home and tell Judy. One way or another everything would slide away and the world would change forever.

He calculated. These cops had no idea who he was. One was near the door. One had him lightly by the elbow. He ran track in high school. If he made it out into the mall, what were their chances of catching him? On the other hand, high school was a while ago. He hadn't run anywhere in years.

"Don't even think about it." The cop placed his free hand lightly on the gun butt sticking out from his hip like a gnarly growth. Danny glanced at the aging pistol. What is he going to do? Shoot me? "I mean it."

The cop was convincing. Danny would get caught sooner or later, and if he got caught, then he would have no excuse at all. For now it was his word against theirs. He was obviously guilty if they had to chase him. And catch him. Danny shuddered.

The second cop finished talking to his walkie-talkie and approached Danny wearing a small grimacing smile as if he had a toothache. He didn't speak to Danny, he didn't even walk directly toward him. He sort of walked behind him.

A ratcheting sound and a movement of arms and something hard like a dog biting his wrist. Danny had not seen the handcuffs, did not even realize they were on him until he pulled his right hand and found his left moved with it.

Danny felt his chest swelling with self-pity. Don't cry, whatever you do, don't cry. He forced himself to speak. "Listen, I was just doing some last-minute shopping." The adrenaline rushed in Danny's veins. He tried to back himself up. "C'mon. Really? Why would I be peeking into a dressing room?" The rush got stronger. Danny felt his face burning.

"That's okay." Nothing was betrayed in the cop's voice, not indictment, nor derision, nor forgiveness.

"It's all . . . it's all . . ." Danny wasn't sure how to finish that sentence. He changed the subject. "Uh, what about my car?"

"You married?"

"What? Yeah."

The cop didn't bother to glance at his partner. "They're always married." The cop checked his beeper stuck onto his belt. Danny remembered his first beeper and how special he felt when he got it. What does a cop need a beeper for?

"Your wife can pick your car up for you."

"No. Listen. I want a lawyer."

"You'll get a lawyer. Don't you worry yourself about that."

Danny focused on the situation. He was very good at dealing with emergencies. He was a very able negotiator. This didn't have to happen. It could stop right now.

"Listen, please, listen to me . . . what's your name, Officer?"

"You have the right to remain silent—"

"Yeah, I know, I know, but listen, wait. . . . *Stop!*"

They paused just inside the doors leading to the parking lot. A few straggling shoppers sensed an unusual rhythm to the policemen's movements and were keeping track from a safe twenty feet away. Danny could see one jowly guy who looked like a neighbor.

"Yeah?"

"You saw her. Come on. Guys. I was just walking by and there she was showing off. What am I supposed to do?"

"Very pretty girl."

"That's what I'm saying! Hey, c'mon, you know? I'm only human."

Danny searched their eyes for pity, for understanding. The only sound was the music from distant speakers wafting through a faint aroma of popcorn and scented candles. Then the second cop, the one who had cuffed him, spoke.

"My niece was raped last year."

The music stopped, Danny felt enormous pressure bearing down, crushing his eardrums, his skin. Even his heart was being flattened.

"I . . ."

A two-way radio crackled and the second cop, his eyes still locked on Danny, picked it up and put it to his lips.

"Yeah?"

Danny heard a garbled something that sounded like "Green eggs and ham."

"Yeah, we're just going out to the car. Figure ten minutes."

He put the radio back down. Danny marveled at the efficiency. They do this all night. They take human beings and ruin their lives all night. Of course they have to be detached about it.

"What's your name?"

"Do I have to tell you my name?"

"What's your name, sir?"

"Danny Marks—I live in West Milford, Maidenbird Lane."

"Mr. Marks, we're going to take you to our headquarters in a few minutes. When we get there you will have your photograph taken and you will be fingerprinted. We'll run your name and Social Security number through the national sex crimes data bank. While we're doing that, you may call your wife or your lawyer. After that, you will be our guest until bail is set by the judge."

The cop broke eye contact and urged Danny out into the hot night air. In a patina of sweat, he found himself standing next to a Crown Victoria with the word POLICE on its side. Someone shoved him and he dropped into the backseat of the cruiser, his wrists laced fast behind him. Danny felt empathy for all the "perps" he had seen on the live cop shows shoved into the backs of cruisers. He liked those shows, but things felt very different from the inside. The burn of the steel girdling his wrists behind his back held him sharply in the moment. The rank aroma of fried food, vomit and urine rising from the woven plastic seat cover crowded his senses. Danny wanted to be home in his study.

15

Shel, Adelle, Terry and Beckett had arranged themselves around one of the dozens of tables scattered into the center of the food court. Terry, long stringy hair, thick glasses, worked out a gothic gargoyle on a napkin with a tiny piece of charcoal as Beckett watched. Adelle, silent, sat looking hurt. Shel babbled.

"Doesn't anyone want to see a movie?"

"What movie?"

"I don't know. That new one, with the, uh . . ."

"With that guy from the TV show?"

"Yeah."

"I hear it sucks."

"Okay." Terry balled up his creation and arced it toward a potted tropical shrub squeezed between the tables. Shel fiddled with each of the five earrings that pierced her left ear, one by one. Beckett chewed a cuticle.

"Why don't we form a suicide pact and kill ourselves?"

"Now that's an idea."

"Yeah, let's do it. Really."

Beckett raked his hair with his fingers. "That's so rad, man. You are such a radical thinker, Terry."

"Blow me." Terry slid his chair backward, squealing metal against the terrazzo floor.

Shel shifted and stretched. "I really need a cigarette. Does anyone want to go out with me while I have a smoke?"

No one looked up when Jeff arrived. He squeezed in between Adelle and Terry.

"Hey."

Adelle smiled up and said nothing. Beckett stood abruptly and snatched at Jeff's arm.

"Come here, I gotta tell you something."

Beckett headed for the rest rooms adjoining the food court. Jeff forced himself from Adelle's orbit. Her eyes followed as he joined Beckett. If Beckett noticed anything between them, he wasn't going to show it.

They passed an angry-looking Slavic janitor rolling a bright yellow mop bucket out the door of the men's. The stench of pine and chemicals hung in the air. Beckett jammed his hand into a back pocket.

"I got it and I'm doing it."

"I was talking to Adelle."

"No you weren't."

Jeff was defiant. "I was about to talk to her."

"What are you going to talk to her about? She's a block of wood. I think she's on some kind of heavy tranquilizer."

Beckett's hand was out of his back pocket and he was thrusting it toward Jeff. A small piece of wrapping paper folded into an origami envelope.

"What is it?"

Like a magician performing a trick, Beckett pulled the tiny envelope open, revealing three minuscule brown rectangles.

"Windowpane, man."

"That's windowpane?"

"Oh yeah."

"Shouldn't a windowpane be clear? Those are brown."

"This is windowpane, dude. This is it. It's like a sheet of dried
gelatin, impregnated with pure godhead, LSD-25."

"Are you going to do some?"

"I already did. About a half hour ago."

"And?"

"Nothing. Too soon to tell."

Jeff kept his eyes locked on the bits of gelatin perched on the
wrapping paper sitting in Beckett's palm. He glanced around for
the janitor.

Beckett licked his lips. "So take one."

"This isn't a good night for that shit."

"Why not?"

"I don't know. I just wanted to hang. Talk to Adelle."

"Fuck Adelle. Adelle is brain dead. What's your thing about
Adelle? She's nobody."

"She's not nobody."

"Have you ever had a conversation with her? She doesn't have
a thought in her head. She just smokes cigarettes."

"And she's extraordinarily beautiful."

"She is?"

"Of course she is!"

"I never noticed how she looked."

The janitor returned. This time he carried a large roll of paper
toweling and a set of small keys. He opened the paper towel dis-
penser with the keys and fitted the roll into it. The janitor walked
out again, never once looking at the boys.

Jeff walked over to the sinks and pressed one of the taps.

"He knows we're up to something. Maybe he's going to get a cop."

"So take one before he does."

"Who else is doing it?"

"I didn't ask anybody else. Shel might freak out or something."

"*I* might freak out or something."

"You've done mescaline, you've done X, you've smoked that green hash I got. It's the same, just stronger." Beckett looked down at his feet and steadied himself. "Oh yeah!"

Jeff knew this was a bad idea. "What? Are you okay?"

"Just got a wave of something. Behind my knees." Beckett's brow furrowed. "Come on, *man,* you gonna let me twist slowly in the wind here? You said if I got it, you'd do it. Now I'm all alone."

"Ask Terry."

"Okay, be like that. Some friend."

Jeff looked down at the tiny squares.

"How do I do it?"

"Wet the tip of your finger. Then touch one."

Jeff picked up the fragment.

"That's it?"

"No, you idiot. Put it in your mouth."

Jeff put the square on his tongue. "How can I swallow this, it's too small."

"Just leave it in your mouth. It'll do what it's supposed to."

Moments later Jeff and Beckett rejoined the group. Terry was organizing his pile of drawings. Adelle sat alone, she didn't look at Jeff. Beckett sat next to Adelle.

Jeff couldn't detect the minuscule square inside his mouth. It seemed ridiculous something so small could affect him at all.

"So what are we doing?"

Terry spoke without looking up. "We can't stay here. They close in about ten minutes."

Jeff glanced at Adelle, now busy listening to Beckett whispering into her small, perfectly formed ear.

Shel came running across the food court, past the empty tables toward the group.

"Something is happening. Check it out! I was having a smoke and these cops came out the doors with this pervert in handcuffs."

"Pervert?"

"A fucking Peeping Tom, man. Guy had been hanging out around the women's dressing rooms at Penney's trying to scope some bush! Security showed up with cops and they busted his yuppie ass. Dragged him outside in handcuffs. Walked right past me."

"He's outside?"

"Yeah. By Penney's."

Terry rose from his chair. Jeff turned to Adelle.

"You coming? Adelle?"

Adelle turned her calm green eyes toward Jeff.

"Yes?"

"You should see this."

"Why?"

"It could be interesting."

Jeff could feel Beckett watching him with detachment. Beckett smiled. His pupils were dilated. Jeff wondered when Beckett had started shaving.

"Maybe later, Jeff, I'm sort of in the middle of something."

"Okay. But don't forget, all right?"

"I won't."

With that, Adelle turned back to Beckett and Beckett smiled at Adelle. The others were already gone. Jeff didn't want to go, but he couldn't stay here.

16

In the glare of the arc lights Mal took the cans from the attendant and fitted them into the dank trunk of his car. As he dropped back into the worn nylon upholstered seat, he didn't concern himself with the police cruiser in his peripheral vision. He knew they wouldn't do anything about some guy being rude. "Catch up with you later, boys."

Rolling off, Mal forced himself to eat. His mental clarity depended on a steady supply of nutrients to his brain cells. His inner child yearned for cookies and milk, so Mal ate the Oreos and drank the half-and-half from the quart container. His mood began to lift. Everything was as it should be. Two pistols strapped to his body, a machine gun beside him, a machine gun on the backseat, two shotguns in the trunk and the bag of shells. The weight of the guns made his soul feel light. Mal felt like the neck of an hourglass. In the next few hours, every grain of time had to pass through him.

Mal's car slipped past the rhumba line of vehicles trying to get out of the mall parking lot. He eased over by the JCPenney and noted the police cruiser with the men standing next to it. Mal rolled past, examining the situation. Cops doing their cop thing. Mal knew these cops, whoever they were, were impressed with themselves for arresting some schmo shoplifting. They had never, ever, encountered what Mal had in store for them.

Mal pulled into a spot near some dumpsters sheltered from the main lot by a low wall. Mal knew these dumpsters, knew the doorways that led to them. For now, he simply popped the trunk lock of the car, put the H&K in the gym bag, got out of the car and headed for the lighted portal of the mall's gateway.

When he reached the plate glass doorways, he could see the white-haired security guard moving toward him, keys in hand. He could see the last shoppers making their way out. The guard eyed Mal but not for long. There was no reason to be suspicious of a man with a gym bag. As far as the guard was concerned, Mal was nightshift on any of the vigils maintained throughout the mall.

Mal entered the recirculated air of the mall corridors. He hadn't been around so many people for a while and their presence hit him like a bad stench. He stopped and watched a couple in matching Day-Glo ski parkas. The guy pushed a stroller beside his wife, pregnant with the next stroller occupant. Mal took in the infant in the stroller. If you stopped and really looked, looked past the big eyes and wet cheeks, what was it? A grub, a human larva lying in its own damp shit.

Multiply this worm by a million. Millions of worms working their way out of millions of womb holes, eager to suck creamy tit milk, growing daily, wailing and naked in the cold smog of a high-tech world. That's all they are. Clusters of blood vessels. Food-tubes. Wriggling and screaming. With only two paths open to them, one leading to middle-class mediocrity, the other to scared-shitless poverty. He was doing 'em all a favor.

17

Donna had eluded the situation with the security personnel. She knew they were hip to what she'd been doing. And so what? They had no choice. They had to let her go. Crashing off the coffee, the cigarettes, the booze and the food, she wandered the halls of the mall, antsy and itchy. The shops' managers had begun their closing routine, pulling heavy Plexi panels halfway shut, choking off the hum. Some dragged tables of merchandise to the front door to block out stragglers.

Security men lingered in doorways, college kids wiped down counters, compact young Mexicans mopped floors. The last shoppers headed for the exits, each toting a loop-handled paper bag as a souvenir of the night's visit. A husband bellowed back at a fat-assed woman, urging her to hurry. Then the canned music evaporated. The sound of her own heels clicking along the emptying passageways pissed Donna off.

All these fingernail-chewing, *Eyewitness News*–watching fuckers sailing home to their little lives. I'm stuck with a limp-dicked ex–varsity star who thinks he's king of the world. Fuck him. I'm the special one. I'm more than special.

Donna caught the eye of a twenty-something sweeping out the front door of Ye Olde Jelly Beane Shoppe. He looked up for a sec and Donna smiled at him. He dropped his eyes and focused on his sweeping. Donna stopped and stood there, smiling.

"Hi."

Not sure what he should do, the kid resumed his sweeping, muttering a hello to the floor. A manager inside the store ambled out to the doorway and watched Donna.

"Help you with something, miss?"

"I need some jelly beans."

"Sorry, we're closed."

"You sure?" Donna tried to beam the impatient manager, but he wasn't buying.

"Uh-huh."

"Well, that's too bad. I'm sure I would have loved licking your beans." Donna flashed one last shot at the kid and whirled away.

Refreshed by her encounter, Donna trotted merrily along, not sure where she was going. Maybe she should get in her car, drive to the airport and take the first plane out. To someplace where no one knew her. South America would be nice. Take the credit cards and run 'em to the max and then disappear. Take on a new identity. Marry a Colombian drug lord.

Donna found the end of the hallway, the giant entrance to Sears, now sealed as tightly as a pharaoh's tomb. She felt her keys in her jacket pocket and caressed them. Her hunger was abating. She was getting sleepy.

As she came to the exits that led out to the parking lot, Donna remembered the lounge at the Ramada Inn across the two-lane. She could sit there for forty-five minutes, knock down one dry martini and go home and things would be fine. Donna pushed out into the fresh air of the parking lot. Just as the warm humidity hit her face, she heard a loud noise behind her in the mall but she kept walking. Whatever it was, she needed a drink.

18

The cops who arrested Danny had walked back into the building and left Danny in the dark quiet of the police car. The police-band radio crackled urgently, but Danny couldn't understand what the dispatcher was saying. A series of numbers hooked up with some street names. "Caucasian male" and "threatening language" was all he could make out. The cops were nowhere to be seen. They obviously didn't think Danny had to be guarded.

It must be around ten o'clock, he thought. Judy is wondering where I am. Maybe the cops'll forget I'm here. Maybe they'll come back and let me go. They'll be laughing and joking, saying they just wanted to put a scare into me, teach me a lesson.

Again Danny considered escape. He could work the door open with his feet, run over to the stand of saplings framing the outer edge of the parking lot. He could figure out how to get the handcuffs off later. He could pay some kid to cut them off. As Danny imagined a *Cool Hand Luke* scenario, he noticed that there were no handles on the doors in this backseat. And the front seat was cut off from the back by a heavy-duty steel screen. He was sealed in. If the cops never came back, he'd be trapped here forever.

He could always kick the windows out. Or smash them with his head. Then squeeze out and drop to the asphalt. He wasn't going to do that right now. Because with his luck he'd get caught smashing the windows and that wouldn't look good. No, the best thing was to sit tight, get to the station house, deny everything and make a phone call.

Danny felt himself splashing around in a sad pool of self-reflection. Well, wherever Judy thinks I might be right now, she could never imagine this. Danny laughed out loud to himself. That strapping young woman was very fine. Her skin was flawless. She'd shown him everything. It was like the most perfect fantasy. She knew what she was doing. When we go to court she'll have to testify. Maybe I'll have her strip in front of the judge. Or maybe she won't show up at all. That won't make any difference because by then it will be too late.

Danny laughed louder. I'm losing my mind. That's good. Insanity might make a good defense. A mental institution would be better than prison. Danny recalled a prison movie he had seen. I'm getting ahead of myself here. They'll have to let me make one phone call and I'll call Warren and he'll get me out. In a couple of hours, Warren and I will be sipping brewskis at his place, laughing about the whole stupid thing. I'll describe the situation. "What's a guy supposed to do? Just walk by?" We'll get drunk and watch *SportsCenter* and he'll advise me to deny everything and it will all work out.

But what about the kids? What will Judy tell them? "Kids, Daddy's a pervert. Daddy is the kind of weirdo everyone hates. You can't be left alone with Daddy anymore." I'll lose the kids. I'll never hold their little hands again. Even if I do get near them, how will I be able to look them in the eyes?

Danny was allergic to something in this cruiser and his sinuses were thickening. When he tried to wipe his nose he realized his hands were no longer available. In fact his right hand was going numb. The pain shocked him out of his crying. Danny became indignant. This is what you pay property taxes for?

I work hard, I make money, I diaper the babies. I don't drink, I pay the credit cards every month on time, never had a late charge, never cheated on Judy. Almost never. Once. Whenever I get those little white cards from the dentist, I make an appointment the next day. I get the oil changed every three thousand miles. I watch my cholesterol. I give money to charity. WHAT THE FUCK DO YOU WANT FROM ME?

God didn't answer. Danny began to inventory his life, trying to find the germ seed of this calamity. Where had he made the wrong turn? By being sexually obsessed? That wasn't his fault. That was life. That was his body. By being curious? Willing to take a risk? Or was it deeper? Was Danny essentially a bad person and everything up to now was a scam? Was it that he hadn't deserved any of this good life, had gotten here by accident? The curtain had been torn away and here he was—a naked weasel, dick in hand, exposed for the whole world to gawk at.

Danny sobbed. It was all so unfair. He was stuck in this smelly backseat of a police car, in pain, dying to piss, with no one to talk to, waiting for something to happen. And whatever happened would be bad. Those cops would come back and have some surprise for him. Push him around.

Cops loved doing that to guys like Danny. They didn't get people like him very often. This was their big chance to get revenge on the "haves" of the world. Maybe they would leave him in the cell with some white-trash psychopath or sodomistic homeboy. What could he do about that? Nothing. Fighting would only make it worse. That would be fitting: to be fucked in the ass because he looked at a cock-tease housewife in the JCPenney dressing room.

Well, "this too shall pass," right? And as it passes, it will take my whole life with it. There were things Danny truly loved: Judy, his kids, his house, his clothes. Golfing on Saturdays, coffee and cinnamon rolls while he worked the phones at the office, driving his Saab 9-5 through the car wash. Losing all these things wouldn't be so bad.

Then he remembered the little dish of warmed nuts and the glass of Scotch and the stewardesses serving them to him. He began to weep again. As he tasted the mucus running down the back of his throat he thought of Judy. If things didn't work out, if Warren couldn't get him off, life would be over with Judy. It was as if she had died. To think, just this morning they had had that argument over how much dishwashing liquid to put into the dishwasher. Danny had left the house tight and seething.

They should not have been arguing. They should have been holding each other, caressing each other. They should have been saying prayers of thanks for their health and their wealth and their wonderful children. Now she was gone. No longer would they brew coffee together, get stuck in traffic together, sit next to each other commiserating on the mediocrity of TV. No longer would they go into the kids' rooms and watch their motionless sleep. No longer would they slide into the sheets, naked, touching, kissing. But they weren't doing that to begin with. That's what started the whole problem!

Danny looked up and found faces peering at him through the glass. He turned away only to find more faces to his left. Teenagers had gathered to watch him suffer.

Danny searched for something to say, something that would save him. Nothing came to mind. Then he heard a sound, a series of sounds, almost like gunfire. He looked at the faces of the youths for an answer, but as he did, they disappeared. He craned his neck to see where they were going and saw them running back to the mall, around the building, leaving Danny alone once more.

I'm dreaming. This isn't happening. Sooner or later I'll wake up. I'll wake up and Judy will be lying next to me and I'll kiss her good morning. Soon I'll be eating my low-fat granola and reading the paper. That's what I'll be doing. Soon. Danny began to cry again.

19

For Michel, it was a matter of pride to remain alert even when boredom was a syrup coating his brain and his feet pulsed with agony. Fifteen minutes ago, the mall had been following its usual rhythms. The evening was wearing down, the shoppers were running out of steam and the crowds were thinning out. As the mall approached closing time, a number of things always happened: short-tempered parents rushed their children, last-minute shoppers ran past and managers or their minions carried the heavy-duty zippered security envelopes of money to the locked slot in the wall of the First National Savings Bank. This was when Michel felt he was of most use. He had no heart in chasing gangs of teens around the mall. They did no harm. But the bags of money needed protection, even when he was dog tired.

Michel scrutinized the girl walking down from the Friendly's. She tried to act as if the paper bag she carried was nothing more than a pair of shoes. Michel knew she had the night's receipts in that bag and he knew how easy it would be for anyone to run up to her, grab the bag and take off with the two or three grand in cash. He smiled at her as she passed and she smiled back. She felt safe because he was there. He was happy she was happy. Michel wanted to be as sturdy and dependable as the poured concrete lying beneath his feet. He'd love to see some crook try to grab that bag. Then the boss would see what kind of man he was.

Michel watched the girl make her way down to the turnoff where the bank sat. One of the local cops who took turns guarding the night deposit would be standing by the bank. Once the girl made the turn she was okay. Of course, the cop might be late or not show.

Michel didn't have to be watching the corridor with his whole mind to see something that did not fit. He spent hours upon hours watching a river of humanity float by. The loping man stood out like an exotic alligator. He did not move like a shopper and he was not carrying a shopping bag.

Michel knew the type. In Haiti these were the lean ones who followed the army around, so hungry they would do anything for a handout. He knew their blood-rimmed eyes and their shiny skin, tight against the bone. He knew that walk, thrusting forward as if a rifle were being pressed into the spine.

Who is this thin man? What is he carrying? A gym bag? Michel had only gotten a glimpse of him as he passed. He could see the man was fit but needed a haircut and a shave. He watched the man's back as it moved away from him. (The bag must be heavy, the way it sags.) Michel thought of bank robbery, but the man was not moving toward the bank, he was moving toward Sears and the corridor that lay just before the store. Nothing was down there but a tuxedo shop, a shoe repair and a small candy store. Nothing worth robbing.

The man turned off down the corridor. There was nothing down there. Michel picked up his two-way radio, clicked it on and spoke.

"Hello, Central, this is Michel at the intersection of A and three and I wish to report a suspicious-looking man has just passed my position."

"Yes, Michel, what? What are you saying?"

Michel tried to be clear and calm. "I'm saying I saw a man who looked like he might be up to something."

"Oh. Haven't they locked the doors yet? Shit! Okay. Well, why do you think he's so suspicious? Is he white?"

Michel didn't like this boss. "Yeah, he's white all right. But he's not wearing normal clothes. He's carrying some sort of bag that may contain a weapon. He turned in at lobby two going north. I can't think why he'd be up there. Please advise."

"Michel?"

"Yes?"

"Stay put. I'll call this in to the police."

"Should I walk down and watch two?"

"No. Stay where you are. If he's carrying a weapon, the police should handle it."

"Okay. Ten-four."

"Ten-four."

Michel watched the entrance to corridor two and bit off a piece of fingernail. He didn't trust the boss. The mall was almost empty. No police seemed to be coming. Michel girded himself. He was ready to do what was needed.

20

Barry was counting his receipts, such as they were. This was not the time of year when much was going on in the tuxedo business. In fact, this was the time of year when Barry usually reconsidered the whole enterprise. In May and June when the money was pouring in, Barry couldn't count it fast enough. But these were the dog days.

Barry never planned to be a businessman. Thirty years ago, when he was a teenager rolling in the mud at Woodstock, he renounced money and business forever. But when he wanted that component stereo system and dinners at the sushi place and eightballs of cocaine, well, all those things cost money. So he started working for his dad. Now Dad was in the condo in Boca and Barry ran the tux joint. He didn't sniff cocaine anymore and had decided sushi was disgusting, but he still liked the money.

He had two stores in two malls. Between the two he kept a nice inventory of tuxes, and when they lost their luster he always found a buyer who could rent them to a shabbier clientele. Not that Barry's clientele was that slick. The whole tux-rental game was built on people who couldn't afford their own tux, mostly students and working stiffs.

What was mildly interesting to Barry was that his two stores had to carry a different set of sizes. Here he did mostly student stuff, so he had to carry dozens of forties up to fifties. The other place dealt with the retired cops and construction guys, extra-large men who needed a tux only twice in their lives—at their own and at their kids' weddings.

That was about as interesting as the rental tux trade got. Sizing and buying and selling and sending out cleaning to get the puke and the champagne stains off. Make a little chump change on the side selling the bow ties with the little hook around back and "special" shoe shine and formal wear suspenders and ruffled shirts.

Barry counted the receipts just as his father had done for thirty-five years and as his brother, who owned a florist's, had at his place. Barry built one day on the back of the last, never really considering how it all added up. He owned his home and his kids were in college. His mother had had a benign tumor removed last year. He liked Chinese food. A while ago he'd had a pointless and awkward affair with the woman who did his books. Even fucked her the night before her wedding, which was a big boost to his ego that made him happy even to this day. But that was over.

So Barry was shocked to see Mal walk into his store, even as he had the keys in his hand to finish the lockup. He recognized the guy instantly, but seeing Mal at this time and place was so incongruous, it didn't figure. So Barry simply stood, as if he were seeing things, and said nothing.

Mal put his bag down and stepped up to Barry, picked the keys from his hand and walked back toward the front doors of the shop. The wake of Mal's rank stench washed over Barry. He started to say something, but thought better and instead shoved the small pile of cash on the counter into the bow-tie box.

Mal turned the key in the hidden console to the left of the doors, and the folding Plexiglas wall that served as a night sheath slid closed. A hard clear wall was formed between Mal and Barry and the rest of the mall. Mal pushed two mannequins into the doorway to enhance the closed look, then stepped over to where Barry stood frozen.

Barry figured he better say something. "Mal? Long time, kid. How long has it been? Ten years? You've really matured."

Mal shoved Barry aside and, reaching under the counter, procured a small keypad.

"What's the code, Barry?"

"Come on, Mal, what are you doing? Robbing me? Here, you need money, take what I've got." Barry shoved the bow-tie box at Mal.

"I don't need money, Barry, tell me the code."

"Five-eight-seven-six, for what it's worth. Look, they got cops in this mall now. They roam around. They'll be here to check on me in a few minutes."

Mal punched in the numbers and, still holding the keys, strode to the front of the store, picked up the gym bag and then, passing Barry, moved toward the back of the store.

"Come here, Barry, I want to show you something." Mal strode to the stockroom.

Barry followed Mal.

"Mal, I don't buy stolen goods."

"I'm not here to do business with you, you fat fuck."

"Well, that's ridiculous. Now, listen, you're getting me angry. Gina's home waiting and I don't have time to fuck around with you. I offered you money, now take it and get out of here before I call the cops. And I *will* call the cops. And Mal, I know you, you were always afraid of the customers, that's why you were a shitty salesclerk. You're a timid bastard. So when the cops come, don't think you can run away."

"When do the cops come?" Mal pushed open the door into the back room.

"They come just about now. Right about now. Any minute. Mal. What's this about? What's in the bag? Drugs?"

They were alone in the stockroom, out of sight of the mall corridor. Mal grabbed Barry's left hand, picked up one of the plastic one-way bands used to bundle clothes and bound his wrist to the chrome clothes rack. Mal's grip was like a clamp. Barry decided the best idea was not to resist, and only muttered an ineffectual "Ow!"

Using the keys he'd taken from Barry, Mal unlocked the back door leading out to the parking lot. The keypad to the right of the door began blinking. He punched in the code and cracked open the door.

"Mal, you're not going to steal these clothes. They're tuxes, for God's sake. They're worthless. What am I saying? You know what? You want to steal them, steal them. I'm insured."

Mal found his car parked outside the door, by the dumpster, as he had left it. He opened the trunk and took out one jug of gasoline. He gently dropped the trunk lid, leaving it ajar.

Mal returned to discover Barry trying to chew the plastic ring off his hand. He stepped past Barry and walked through the store, pouring gasoline on the carpeting and the racks of tuxes.

"Hey!" Mal heard a muffled voice.

Mal looked up. Two cops were standing outside the Plexiglas, watching him. Mal put the can down, smiled, waved to the cops and gave them the "one minute" hand signal. He walked back to the stockroom where Barry was held prisoner. Barry's eyes were black with fear, his forehead wet.

"The cops are here," Mal informed Barry.

"Listen, you got what you wanted, you got money. Now the cops are here and you're going to be in a lot of trouble. Just let me go. Walk out the back door and let me go and we'll forget the whole thing. I'll say I don't know who did it."

"You want a second chance, Barry?"

"'Second chance'? Yeah, yeah, Mal, that's what I want."

"Why should I give you a second chance, you fat fuck? Remember the day you fired me? You didn't give *me* a second chance. You didn't think about how you were ruining *my* life."

"Ruining your life? You didn't *have* a life. You were a twenty-two-year-old clerk in a tuxedo rental store. How was firing you ruining your life? You were on drugs, Mal. Looks like you still are. You were skimming my cash! What did you expect me to do? Give you a medal?"

Mal pulled the little .22 pistol from his pocket.

"Oh shit, Mal, come on. Get serious! What are you going to do with that?"

The police were banging on the Plexiglas.

"They're gonna break that door now. Let me go talk to them. And you can leave."

With a box cutter Mal sliced the ring off Barry's wrist. "Go ahead. Tell them what you want to tell them."

Barry rubbed his wrist and watched Mal warily. "I smell gasoline, Mal."

"Go ahead."

As Barry stepped forward, Mal took the little pistol and shot him in the heel.

"Shit! God! What are you doing?"

Barry bolted for the Plexiglas wall, limping on his damaged foot. The cops looked puzzled as he hopped toward them.

"Hey, this guy in here is nuts! He just soaked the store with gasoline. He tied me up. And then he shot my foot."

Through the stockroom doorway, Mal could see Barry appealing to the cops. He unzipped the gym bag, took out his Heckler & Koch submachine gun, dropped to one knee and sighted. The first volley sprayed Barry's back. Barry fell, the Plexiglas shattered and both cops dropped as well. Since Mal had a clear sight to the floor, he had no problem spraying the cops as they instinctively crouched down.

In movies, in a situation like this, the display counters and clothing and tables would fragment and catch the bullets. But that wasn't the way it worked. The bullets had no problem piercing the clothes, piercing the wood paneling, through the Plexiglas and on into the soft flesh of the policemen. Bullets were powerful things.

Mal stepped forward and walked through the reeking store. Neither Barry nor the cops moved. For the hell of it, he unholstered his .38 and pumped a bullet through the back of each immobile head. As he did, the recoil traveled up into his arm, up his spine and through his skull, making a chain reaction of speed-jostle. For a second, Mal's head swam. He stood before the shattered Plexiglas wall, pistol in hand, bodies bloody and awkward at his feet. He reached into his jeans and pulled out his tinfoil package, deftly unfolded it using only his left hand and brought it up to his nose. He inhaled a huge snuffle of devil dust, pure crank, harsher and more intense than the slow but sure beauties. His adrenaline was redlining, so the crank had the effect of making his head throb intensely. As if he were God's crack pipe itself, he hollowed out and filled up with seething fire. He squared his shoulders and howled at the acoustical ceiling tiles.

The pieces were falling together perfectly. From this point onward they could only fall in sequence, there was no other way for this to work out. Mal's plan was without flaw. Fucking Barry wanted him to have pity on him. After what Barry did to Mal, that was a real stretch. One thing Mal prided himself on, he never forgot a transgression. He didn't forgive and he didn't forget. If you cross me, I'll wait, and it may not be today and it may not be tomorrow, but sooner or later I will get you. I will get you and I will find you. And I will fuck you.

Mal hadn't felt this happy in years. He wanted to pull out his other pistol and just shoot the place to pieces. But then he caught something out of the corner of his eye. A movement. Down the corridor outside the shop. Alert as an eagle, Mal aimed one eye at the juncture of the side corridor with the main mall and saw the movement again. Something dark and round was out where the corner met the floor. It got larger. It had eyes. Eyes were watching him. It was the head of a man peeking around the corner.

Mal could have fired at that head and shot that head, but instead, he turned and made his way back through the store. Just as he was about to enter the storeroom, he turned and, pulling a pack of matches from his pocket, lit a Lucky and tossed the lit match onto a pile of clothes. A moment passed before the *whoosh* of igniting gasoline fumes. Two moments later, the entire store was ablaze in an inferno of synthetic material. Mal walked through the storeroom and out the back door.

21

Michel slowly counted to twenty. No movement or sound came from the storefront. His back and his crotch were damp with sweat, his mouth had no moisture. As he stood from his crouch around the corner, the radio babbled on his hip.

"Michel? What's going on?"

The dispatcher no longer sounded impatient and patronizing. Something new was in his voice.

"I don't know, sir. There was shooting. I'm walking over." He could smell the fumes as he saw the flickering light.

The radio went silent, expectant. Michel approached the figures lying zigzag in the shattered Plexiglas, their heads leaking blood, their hair dark and wet. Beyond them the silent flames rolled up inside the store's walls. The fumes grew stronger. The radio blurted something.

"What did you just say, Michel? Who's shot?"

Michel didn't have to turn them over to know that their faces were mangled. He didn't want to see. As he stepped to avoid the blood, tiny cubes of glass crunched under his aching feet.

"They are dead, sir."

"Who?" The voice notched higher, panicked.

Michel eyed the interior of the store as if the answer lay there. He had seen the man with the gym bag holding a gun. The man could be aiming at him ready to shoot now. The man had disappeared into the store, into the fire. Was he there, burning? Cautiously, Michel stepped through the smashed Plexi wall and into the store proper.

Inside, Barry, the owner, lay beside the two broken guardian mannequins. Michel had seen the tux man many times on his daily pilgrimage to McDonald's. Barry had a black spot in the center of his temple and his face was pinched and angry. His stomach and legs had quarter-size marks on them. No pulse coursed in the holes puddled with blood.

"Three are dead, sir. Two policemen and the owner of the store. And the store's on fire."

"Michel, what are you talking about? Speak slowly, I can barely understand you! Speak English!"

Michel squinted into the rear. Like yellow-red imps, the flames ran over the racks of clothing. The burning, glossy synthetics burped out clouds of funereal smoke. Michel allowed himself the luxury of thinking what a pleasant job it would be to work in this place. To be able to dress nicely every day, to be able to converse with people, help them with their selections. He wondered what the pay was like. The two-way crackled.

"Michel . . . what?" The boss sounded more and more urgent.

"The store is on fire, sir."

"Well, Michel, just wait there. I called it in."

Michel waited. He didn't look at the bodies. He had seen bodies many times before. He knew a bad magic lived in a body killed by extreme violence. Such a corpse contained a toxic message and if a person looked at the body for more than a second or two, the poison left the body and seeped into the viewer's soul. Knowledge of the frailty of life inflated the guts and strangled the heart.

Michel remembered the women in white, dancing, muttering the gibberish of the ceremony. He remembered the fear everyone shared of the dead not staying in their graves. The incantations, the blood sacrifices, the smell of sweat and the swirling dancers all came back to him. He wished his *maman* were here right now so he could bury his close-cropped skull in her skirts as he had done then. The dead don't sleep unless they are forced to. He knew their spirits were here right now watching him. He whispered a church prayer under his breath.

The man with the gym bag was back there somewhere. Any opportunity to stop the man was burning up as fast as the store. Michel could feel the dead men behind him, imploring him to seek justice. If he waited a moment longer, their fingers would come up behind him and . . .

Michel grabbed a dress shirt off a shelf, tore off its cellophane wrapping and, crumpling it up, held the starchy pink cloth to his face. He walked deeper into the store, toward the back. The murderous smoke hung in the air like black cotton, waiting for him. The man with the gym bag was back there, Michel would find him.

"Michel, you're not doing anything, are you? Don't do anything. I'm sending Joey down. Don't touch anything."

"Yes, sir."

Michel gently switched his two-way off and lay it on a table of rectangular, clear plastic boxes, each containing one bow tie. Mirrors on all sides filled with bright flame and the dark fumes fogged the recessed lighting.

Michel ducked down and stepped forward into the orange-tinted gloom. This must be what it's like to walk with Satan through hell, he thought. A glossy poster of a square-jawed man in powder blue formal wear smiled at Michel as he passed into the back room. The man's smile became a grimace as the paper shrank and twisted in the heat.

In the back, there were no flames to illuminate the darkness. Michel could feel the cool air of the parking lot. It was moving in from the open door in the back wall. The man with the gym bag had escaped.

Michel understood with crystalline clarity what he should do. Find the man. Stop the man. Before he could choke it off, he said the words as well as he could remember them: *"Atibô-Legba, l'uvri bayè pu mwê, agoé! Papa-Legba, l'urvi bayè pu mwê, pu mwê pasé."* If black magic was what it took, then so be it, let the *loas* help him.

22

Jeff tried to arrange his crowded thoughts. He was having difficulty distinguishing between the sights and sounds of the mall and what was happening to his nervous system. According to Shel, a man had been arrested for peeping in the dressing rooms at the JCPenney and was now handcuffed in a cruiser outside. They had all gone to look at him sitting in the little cave of the cruiser's backseat. All Jeff could think was how miserable and crushed the man had looked.

Fire trucks were arriving as Jeff cycled through these thoughts. Also down by Penney's. Perhaps the voyeur had set the fire. Would that be possible if he was handcuffed in the back of the cruiser?

This was a lot of information to be processed. More in five minutes than Jeff normally had to handle in a few days. Jeff was trying to wrangle the significance of all these things happening at the same time. He couldn't. He couldn't tell if he couldn't because there was no significance at all or because he was tripping on acid. Maybe these were normal events and they only felt unusual because he was high. After all, fire trucks did exist, and they wouldn't exist if there weren't fires often enough to justify their expense. Otherwise what would the firemen do all day? Probably acid. Jeff chuckled to himself. He tried to peel apart what he had seen and heard, attempting to create two compartments in his brain, one labeled "normal" and the other labeled "unusual." He further dissected the moment by discerning what was "inside" and what was "outside." He went a step further and separated what was a "thought" and what was a "feeling." Then he lost track of what he was thinking altogether.

Jeff looked up to see Adelle walking toward him, alone. She almost seemed happy to see him. Confusion balled and writhed in Jeff's stomach. He looked down at his belly to see if it was, in fact, writhing. There was movement.

"Hey." Adelle stopped and stood next to Jeff. Jeff looked up at her. Adelle turned away. Jeff stood. Somehow he found himself holding a lit cigarette and smoking it.

Jeff and Adelle stood wordless beside each other, smoking. Fire trucks arrived via the interstate, down the mall road, down the ramps, sliding around the corner of the building one by one. Jeff could see the impassive firemen in their seats, dressed in black raincoats and black hats.

"Don't firemen wear red?" he asked.

"What?" Adelle looked away and exhaled.

"Don't firemen wear red? Those firemen are wearing black."

"Fire trucks are red," Adelle observed calmly.

"Oh. I always thought firemen had red outfits. When I was small, I had a fireman's hat and it was red."

"Really? You had a fireman's hat? Do you still have it?"

Jeff wasn't sure if she was mocking him. "Do you think the mall is on fire?"

"Probably."

"Adelle?"

"What?"

"Nothing. I just wanted to say your name."

"Don't get weird on me, Jeff. Are you doing that acid Beckett is doing?"

Jeff felt as if his clothes had been stripped off his body. What else did she know? Goose bumps rose on his hot skin.

"Yes."

"Yeah, Beckett told me. Why are you doing that?"

"I'm tripping."

"Yeah, but why? Isn't that kind of stupid?"

"Stupid? How?"

"Well, first of all, aren't you afraid of losing your mind?"

"No." Jeff's voice sounded very small to him. He wondered if it sounded small to Adelle. This might be the most important moment of his life. He cleared his throat and said firmly: "No."

"Why are you shouting? Is it because you're tripping?"

"I don't think I'm tripping yet. I'm not sure."

"My older brother had a friend who did acid all the time. The guy became schizoid."

"Schizoid?" Was that a word?

"Yeah. He's in an institution now. In Massachusetts. He's never coming out."

"Oh. Well, this isn't that kind of acid, I don't think. The schizoid kind."

"Acid is acid. I'd never do it in a million years."

"A million years is a long time, Adelle. A lot can happen in a million years."

"Oh wow, man, heavy."

"Can we change the subject?"

"Sure. Just don't start freaking out on me. I wouldn't know what to do."

A riptide of fear was pulling Jeff into deeper water. There was a right and a wrong thing to say here. He wished he knew what it was.

"Are you going to college in the fall?" Jeff hated the words as soon as he uttered them.

"No."

"Me neither."

"I'm moving to New York. I'm going to model." Adelle snuffed out her cigarette with an angry twist of her toe.

"Oh."

"I look at it this way, they always need new models. You don't have to be pretty in the old-fashioned way anymore. You can be 'interesting looking.' I figure the worst I can do is end up doing porno videos." Adelle lit a fresh butt and exhaled a stream of white smoke.

"What?"

"I said the worst I can do is porno. Does acid make you go deaf?"

"That would be horrible. More than horrible."

"I'm joking, asshole."

"Oh. Wait, I was thinking about something."

"That's good. Are they ever coming back? Maybe we should go look at the fire? I bet they're by the fire."

"No, but Adelle, you *are* pretty. You're more than pretty."

"Thanks."

"I'm not saying it just to say it. I think you're the prettiest girl among all the girls . . . uh, women I know."

"You do?" Her eyes widened with genuine curiosity.

"Yeah."

"Do you mean that?"

"Yeah. I know you're joking about doing porno and everything but it would be an incredible tragedy if you were to, you know, do anything that compromised your beauty."

Adelle gazed blankly at Jeff. He wasn't used to her giving him her complete attention like this. There was a constriction somewhere. His chest? His crotch? He couldn't tell.

"Jeff, are you saying you like me?"

"Yeah."

"Like you want to go out with me?"

"Yeah."

"And fuck me and stuff?"

"Huh?"

"Is that what you're saying?"

"Adelle, yes, I like you. Yes. I'm happy to be near you." Jeff wished she would stop talking. Let the moment shimmer with its potential beauty. He only wanted to love her.

"And fuck me and stuff?"

"I don't know."

"You don't know?"

"Wait a second, you're messing with my head, right?"

"No. I want to know if you want to fuck me and stuff."

"'And stuff'?"

"You know."

"Adelle, this is weird what you're saying."

"Why is it weird? You just said I'm the prettiest girl you know, which makes me think you like me, and when a guy likes a girl, he wants to fuck her. Right?"

"Yeah, but . . ."

"And stuff . . ."

Panic seized Jeff. "What 'stuff' are you talking about?"

"You know, blow jobs and rim jobs and licking your balls and stuff like that. Getting down doggie-style. Like in the song?"

"Adelle, stop. Please?"

"Don't you want me to lick your balls?"

"No!!!"

"Why not?"

"I don't know! I just want to hang with you and hold you."

"Why?"

"Because I'm in love with you, that's why. Okay? Wow."

Jeff sat down on the curb.

"You want another cigarette, Jeff?"

"No."

Adelle sat down next to Jeff. "What's a matter, did I hurt your feelings?"

"No. I just never . . . we never talked before."

"Do you really love me?"

"C'mon!"

"Do you?"

"Yeah."

"You don't like it that I said 'rim job'? Do you even know what a 'rim job' is, Jeff?"

"Of course I know what a rim job is."

"What is it?"

"Adelle . . . stop!"

"Jeff, are you a virgin?"

"No."

"Jeff, can I tell you something and promise you won't get mad?"

"I won't get mad."

"You're really unexciting."

Adelle stood up, stubbed out her cigarette and walked away, leaving Jeff on the curb. Jeff watched her get swallowed up by the heat of the parking lot. He was on the very edge of a very deep hole and, leaning back, away from the maw, he involuntarily looked up. Overhead the night sky was an irritating black velvet and the stars white laser pointers drilling into his skull. The orange glow on the periphery of his vision seemed to be closing in on him, taking his breath away.

Adelle had been hurt in a very deep way. Sorrow lay in the marrow of her bones. Jeff could see it in her face. If his sorrow could speak to her sorrow there would be poetry. Instead she had turned away from her sorrow. The conversation hadn't gone the way it should have. He hadn't said the right things. She had talked trash just to shock him, to push him away, to build a wall between them because she was frightened. She hadn't recognized her soul mate.

Jeff turned around and looked at the mall building. Above the red outline of the silhouetted building, a long whip of red flame lashed up into the air. The tongue licked the sky and lit up the smoke billowing over the roof. Jeff thought he heard a vast laugh.

More sirens were approaching, now police cars, ambulances. Chaos was happening. This frenzy was reaching out to Jeff and trying to grab him, *was* grabbing him. His despondency fell away like a thin paper shroud, crumpled up and disappeared. Jeff forgot what he was upset about.

23

Mal had an advantage over everyone else because he knew what he was going to do and they didn't. He gazed out through his windshield and inhaled a Lucky.

This was all a person could ask for in life. To touch others, mess with their destiny. Otherwise a person just came and went, as if he were never alive in the first place. Mal's shadow days were over. Mal had tossed a hook deep down the world's throat, was reeling it in and it couldn't get away.

Besides, Barry was a fat fuck worthless to anybody. Barry thought he was better than Mal. That had always been obvious. So Mal was happy to kill his blubbery ass, even if no one ever knew.

Mal knew he stank, but he liked the smell. The smell reminded him of the drugs, which reminded him of the store burning behind him and Barry's fat body. He smiled. Maybe Barry's fat was sizzling right now, melting, cooking, getting nicely charred. A smaller ripple traversed his skull. Maybe I should go back and hack off a piece and eat it?

Mal ignored a fissure of pain that shot up inside his right temple. Agony, loose teeth and perpetually wet skin—speed's phantom crucifixion was the price you paid.

A police cruiser rounded the turn and flared its searchlight onto the dumpsters and then found the car where Mal sat. The cruiser stopped. The searchlight went out. Nothing happened for a moment, then the cruiser, in an act of caution, backed up twenty feet. The ten-thousand-candle searchlight snapped on again and saturated Mal, blinding him. Mal looked down at his lap. A voice, filtered through a mini-PA, chopped out a few words.

"Step out of the vehicle with both hands in sight!"

Mal blinked his headlights in acknowledgment, popped his door and slowly, methodically, stepped out of the car. Yeah, Mal knew the drill. Stupid fucks. He stood with the open car door between him and the police vehicle forty feet away. He faced the cops and raised his hands. Mal shouted over to them in a "just between us guys" voice. "I'm waiting for my sister to get out of work!"

"Step away from the vehicle."

Mal began to move. Everything slowed, he became the all-seeing eye. Something like love flitted through his chest. He knew where they were, he knew who he was, he knew what he could do. They didn't and for that ignorance he loved them. He had seen the pope once on TV. The pope would give Communion to the lucky and, as he did, would nod and smile the smallest, most benign smile. Mal felt that gentle smile on his lips.

Mal let all the muscles in his arms, legs and back relax. He wilted behind the open door of his car. Then like a cobra striking, he picked up the H&K, punched on his high beams and, dropping the machine gun into the crack between the car body and the open door, stung the cruiser with fifty rounds in a short burst. Before the police could return fire, Mal dumped the gun back into the front seat and scurried to the rear where the trunk was already ajar. They had no idea who he was and that was a beautiful thing. Meet God.

Taking a shotgun in each hand like some kind of Warner Brothers hero, he scuttled ten feet to one side, shotgunning the cop car. Then, protected by the deep shadows of the thick iron–walled dumpsters, he finished his work, pumping until the drops of sweat salted his eyes.

The searchlight, the doors, the windows and the cops within shattered. The punctures spat blood and gasoline. Blinking with excitement, Mal stepped back to his car, threw the guns back into the trunk and slammed it. That was that. The kaleidoscope rush of adrenaline was terrific.

Mal got back into his car and shoved the H&K over on the seat. He didn't have to look at the cruiser, he knew what he'd find. Turning to see all was clear, Mal caught the back door of the tuxedo store opening and the large silhouette appear in it.

"Oh, yeah, 'the Head.' Well, see ya later, 'Head.'"

Mal pulled out his .38 and sighted on Michel. He only had time for one shot. He squeezed the trigger and stepped on the gas.

24

Donna sat at the bar of the Ramada Inn working on a vodka martini. Most everyone who came to this lounge occupied the little brown tables and chairs with the fake-o colonial brass-studded red leather trim. The bar itself was the domain of the bartender and the waitress in her black outfit.

So Donna sat alone. The men at the tables, under the golden glow of the plastic Tiffany-esque mini-chandeliers, their wives an arm's length away, appraised the woman at the bar. Not that any one of them could do anything about their curiosity. They were following the path of least resistance—shopping with their spouses, having a quick drink with them while discussing their mothers and brothers and other sources of irritation, followed by a quick meal of "surf 'n turf" in the dining area. ("And would you like sour cream and chives with your baked?") Afterward, a three-traffic-light cruise would bring them back to their snug half-paid-for home, twenty minutes worth of Jay Leno and bed. No room anywhere for Donna, other than fantasy.

Oblivious, Donna focused on getting the alcohol into her

bloodstream. In her gut a rage was building, a deep, nasty dissatisfaction. She tried to maintain a sunny disposition most of the time. She tried to be the clucking mom the kids needed. She did her best as the supportive, fellating wench Roy required to get it up. She cleaned the house, sort of. She read magazines. She attempted interest in what seemed to interest all the other women. But she wanted more!

Donna could hear the sirens and the growing chatter among the table-bound behind her. Something was happening at the mall, a fire. Two of the men were standing at the window watching. Donna could think of better things to do than stand and goggle at the fire trucks. Maybe if she had at least three drinks in her belly, she could check out the firemen. She hunched over her vodka and watched the silent TV set hanging over the Plexi nacho chips case.

Thoughts rattled into Donna's skull like freight cars in a trainyard. The guys would be home by now. Roy would be building up his patronizing attitude. She should call him. She should call him right now. Before he could work on Roy Jr. No. He'd just have to fend for himself. She was out shopping. She had a right. She saw his patronizing smirk in her mind's eye. Okay. Okay. One more drink and then push off. She focused on the TV by the barkeep's head.

Two boxers were fighting onscreen. Donna appreciated how slick and well-lit they were. They seemed to be Mexican. One guy was taller and spent most of his time with his gloves up and his elbows down, letting the other guy punch himself out. The announcers prattled on about the superior technique of the taller, more cautious guy.

But the shorter one, who featured a rattail braid running down between his defined deltoids, was not running out of energy. He kept bouncing on the balls of his feet, letting his left arm hang limp, his right fist circling, warning of a hard hook. But he saved his right, left it as a diversion. Instead, his unlikely left would shoot up and out with jack-rabbit speed over and over, finding holes in the well-protected face and ribs of his opponent. Whenever the wary taller guy returned with a jab, the little guy would dance backward, or simply tilt his head away, making it look easy. The little guy kept bobbing and smiling, looking in and ducking back, raising his right fist and then shooting out with his left.

The taller guy made his move—a strong, straight jab right to the little guy's head. But the little guy's head wasn't there when the gloved fist arrived. Finally the little guy did it, finally let his right hook go. Like the boy who cried wolf, the roundhouse punch came, doing what it had threatened all along. With a spray of sweat and spit, the tall guy crumpled, KO'd flat on the canvas.

I like that little guy, thought Donna. Why can't I find a guy like that?

25

Michel watched the culprit's automobile ease off into the pastel gloom of the mall parking lot. The car did not aim for the mall exit, rather drifted off into a dim patch on the far end of the lot, until all Michel could see were the red taillights floating on the black edges of the asphalt plain. Then they disappeared as well.

The flames from within the store warmed Michel's back, urging him out into the night. The door swung closed behind him and Michel turned and looked at it. The bullet had pierced the door exactly at the height of his heart.

Michel stepped forward, straining to see a flicker of the car, but it was gone. To his left, no movement came from the ruined police cruiser. The radio in the car made a clicking noise, but that was all, a transmission from station STYX. Michel did not want to see any more dead people tonight, so he turned away. As he did, his large aching foot nudged a hard object lying on the ground.

Reaching down Michel felt something cool, smooth and hard. He knew what it was. He could smell its tang. He picked it up, looked around and without another thought, lay the barrel against his leg and walked away from the building, past the torn-up police car, toward the middle of the lot where only a few lonely vehicles stood parked.

Trembling, Michel found a spot between two cars and in the faint light, alone, he dared to examine his prize.

This shotgun was different than others Michel had handled. He'd heard of this type. "Auto." His thick fingers found the latch and cracked the breech. One fat red-and-brass shell sat ready. Michel had no way of knowing if there were others behind it. Somehow the gun, with at least one live shell in it, had missed finding its home in the trunk of the car. In his fury, the skinny man had not noticed.

Michel believed in God, the saints, the *loas*. Despite what had happened to Marie, despite his tribulations, despite the nastiness he had seen in Haiti, he believed. God in his wisdom and majesty had placed poor Michel in this place at this time and put this gun in his hand. It was the only explanation. Michel knew what to do with a shotgun, oh yes, he knew shotguns well. He had wielded them. He had seen blasted bellies cauliflowered with fat and blood. He would do God's work and find this skinny piece of bone and gristle, this gym bag man, and he would use the shotgun on him. Michel would be redeemed. Michel would find grace and satisfaction whatever it took.

Michel made the sign of the cross over his face and chest, snapped the shotgun back together, laid it against his leg and, without a glance back at the fire trucks, walked toward the edges.

26

Danny curled up in the murk. His life was over because of one mistake. He'd always thought of himself as a lucky guy, always felt that of all the lives he'd want to lead the one he had gotten would have been his choice. Perhaps this was the payback. Perhaps everyone gets payback one way or the other. It's a zero-sum game. If things are good now they're going to be bad in the future. If they're bad—for instance, you're born with a terrible disfigurement—then later in life you get what you always—

Danny interrupted himself because this was bullshit. It didn't work that way. Some people got the brass ring and some people got fucked. Maybe he'd been mistaken—maybe he was one of the fucked. Maybe this is fate. Maybe this is just the way things were meant to work out. Big surprise! Your life isn't great, your life sucks. No pain, no gain.

One of the cops had returned. The door opened and fresh air flooded the interior.

"Something has come up. I'm going to uncuff you and give

you a ticket for a court appearance. We don't have the time tonight to take you in."

"What happened?" Danny's voice twittered like a bird's.

"I'm not sure. Something bad. A fire. And . . . uh . . . I'm not free to say. You're a lucky guy, look at it that way."

The cop took a key out of his pocket, then leaned into the back of the car. He tried to reach around to unlock Danny's cuffs.

"Maybe it would be easier if I got out?" Danny's heart raced with gratitude.

"Yeah." The cop sounded distracted.

Danny heard a pop. Must be one of those teenagers screwing around, popping paper bags. The policeman froze for a moment with a funny smile on his face. Danny thought, Good. He'll go chew out those kids for spying on me.

With a sigh, the cop melted onto Danny. Was the guy still trying to reach around him? This was a strange way to do it. Had he passed out? As Danny tried to push up on the weight, he felt something like warm water spilling onto him. The cop is pissing on me, he thought. But the cop was not moving.

"Hey? You okay?" Danny craned his neck to see where the kids went. They were gone. He was alone with the mute, immobile cop. And he was wet.

Then a tall, skinny man appeared before the car. Danny could see the guy, but was pretty sure, being covered by the cop, he was invisible. The man was holding a large red plastic jug and was splashing something all over the hood of the cruiser.

Danny considered calling out to the tall man, and then the man made an elegant move with his arm, a flourish like a magician. Flame shot out of his fingers. As the man walked away, the grille and hood of the cruiser ignited with a pleasingly soft *poof.*

The cop on top of me is dead. I am in a burning police car. Instantly, Danny pushed up hard against the cop's fresh corpse and muscled him out the door. The body flopped onto the pavement outside and Danny shimmied himself out the now open back door. He knew that according to TV crime show lore, if he did not get out of the cruiser within twenty seconds, the entire metal box would blow up, cooking him like a trout in tinfoil.

The hood and grille of the cruiser were a tangle of sinuous flame. Danny straightened up for the first time in an hour and limped away toward the mall. As Danny caught his breath, he found he couldn't get his arms from behind his back and he remembered the cuffs. The cop was about to unlock his cuffs. Which meant that the cop had the key to the cuffs. In his hand?

Soon the burning car would become a metal bonfire and Danny would never be able to get to the key. Trussed like this, he couldn't go anywhere without drawing attention to himself. No good. He had to get the key. He inched back toward the car. He paused three feet from the cop. The body was lying on its back on the blacktop next to the rear right tire, the arm laid out at an angle. The hand was empty.

Danny searched in the flickering light. Nothing on the ground. He checked the backseat of the cruiser, his own private hell just a few minutes before. In the footwell lay something small and silver.

Danny stepped forward, over the cop's body. As he did, a bulging dollop of flame expanded through the steel mesh and back into the car. Danny felt the skin on his face tighten. He did an about-face and, with his back to the floor, squatted down just outside the car. Raising his arms backward, he reached for the key. He leaned back as far as he could as the flames from the front formed a bridge of fire over his face.

This is why they cuff you behind your back, he reasoned. From Danny's perspective, lying backward across the floor of the cruiser, facing upward, the fire was a hungry animal scrambling toward the rear where the gas tank lay.

I'm going to get blown up in this police car. Burned alive in handcuffs. Somewhere, far away, he could hear the police dispatcher frantically calling. The lining of the roof had ignited and as Danny looked up, droplets of melting fabric dripped shimmering onto him. He gave up and with a shove pushed himself out of the car, onto his knees, onto the stomach of the dead cop. The body wheezed. Danny smelled shit.

God, please! Danny struggled to his feet and again staggered away from the car. A dozen steps later the flames finally found the fumes of the gas tank. A *boom*. The heat multiplied exponentially. Danny felt a tickle along his spine as his clothing caught on fire. My jacket is on fire. My jacket is on fire. Educational fire safety filmstrips ran inside his skull. He fell to the ground and rolled onto his back, trying to smother the burning. Wrenching his arms, pulling his shoulder bones out of their sockets, the metal cut deeper and deeper into his bound wrists. He couldn't be sure the fire was out, so he kept writhing, only mutilating his wrists more.

Lying on his battered arms, not sure the small blaze on his back was extinguished, Danny pulled himself up and crawled off like a whipped dog. Seeing the decorative evergreens by the JCPenney entrance, he crept behind them and hid.

If I get these handcuffs off, I can go home and no one will know what happened. Judy will wonder about my clothes but I'll say the car broke down and uh . . . it doesn't make any difference what I say. Just get home. Just get home. Get me home, God, and I promise, God, I will never touch my dick again. In his shelter of irrigated pine, Danny lay still and, despite the savage pain in his wrists, lay his face onto the chipped cedar bark mulch and passed out.

27

Jeff had found his way to the fire that centered around a cluster of dumpsters. Frigid, rock-hard canvas hoses snaked into the back door of one store. Piles of smoking tuxedos lay stacked on the asphalt, the air spiced with the scent of many burned things. Jeff could also see the flames had found their way to the tar and gravel top of the building. Water dribbled off the roof and formed pools at the firemen's feet. Everyone shouted to everyone else. It could have been a Saturday afternoon scrimmage.

Jeff sat down. Waves of euphoria broke over him. He casually took in the trailing iridescent colors, the echoing sounds. On the roof, the flames jumped up like mad cheerleaders as if on cue. Jeff smiled to himself. This is something I can tell my children about. The night the mall burned down. I'm watching history, man. I'm part of history!

As Jeff attempted to put a narrative to the scenario, two men passed him walking a covered gurney to the ambulance. He contemplated the efficiency of a stretcher on wheels. Then, with a shiver, Jeff understood he was watching a corpse being handled.

He grounded himself with a little mantra: "This is not TV. Not TV. Not TV."

Jeff stood and wandered over to where the gurneys waited beside the idling, light-churning ambulance. Blotches of color swam over the bedded shapes. Unsmiling men, all sporting dark, clipped mustaches, murmured in low tones reviewing in detail what had happened and what was going to happen. Now Jeff could see behind the fire engines and ambulances. A disfigured police cruiser, ragged with ugly holes, tires flat, oil and antifreeze puddled under its belly, stood dead.

Jeff couldn't hear everything being said but he heard the word *he* and followed the angry pointing fingers toward the woods tucked in by the interstate. The radio on one man's hip crackled. A glance, a word, and four of the men peeled off. Two remained by the draped bodies.

Jeff crept closer. He stood by the men, as if he had a purpose here. In this tragedy all men were brothers, all united against the threat, even freaks like himself. The sheet was pulled aside. Jeff looked down. At first all he could see was the sprawling rent in the corpse's temple where the bullet had emerged, pushing his brow down over his eyelids. It was an awesome topography, as abnormal as a mutant birth. Jeff felt tricked. This is a hoax, he thought, a rubber Halloween mask. Then Jeff saw the blond mustache, a glimmer of green pupil. And he knew whose body he was looking at.

The asphalt of the parking lot tipped. Jeff stepped away, past the ambulance, past the firemen pulling hoses, past the squat dumpsters and off to somewhere, he wasn't sure where. An edge. A safety zone where bad things didn't happen. He felt like he was on fire himself. Life, which had been a simple ideological battle fifteen minutes ago, had become an impossible and scary nightmare. He didn't want to be tripping anymore.

Jeff moved across the expanse of the evacuated parking lot. He didn't see the cars gliding past him, drawn like moths to the flame. When the driver of the TV van asked him what was going on, he didn't have an answer but kept walking. He forgot about his friends. Terror nuzzled and nipped at him like a playful hellhound.

There were lights ahead. The lights were in ordered lines, making sense, promising a better world. Jeff rushed toward them. He didn't know what he would find there, but he needed the embrace of the friendly glow. He needed the order and assurance of the mundane. He needed to stop thinking.

28

A dozen cops milled around their collection of official and unofficial vehicles, watching the firemen do their work. Most only wanted to go home to their wives and kids and split-levels with a view of the barbecue in the backyard. They had been cops for years and had never seen one of their own killed. Suburban police work was a job. You don't get killed for a paycheck. Five cops was a lot of cops. Any one of them could be next.

Some were angry enough to be grateful because they had weapons and the right to hunt this killer down. They didn't have to ask anybody's permission. They didn't need a warrant. They could find this guy right now and shoot him on the spot and it would be okay.

The men came to a decision. They would drive slowly over to the side of the parking lot where some kids had said they saw a car. The side where the tree stand was. Beyond the five acres of skinny maples and poplar was a rise, and on top of the rise, the interstate highway. They'd put two cars on the interstate in case he tried to run across. They would trap him in the trees.

Heads nodded in unison. One man dared speak. "What if he shoots at us?"

"Then we shoot back and retreat. We'll know where he is and we'll have him cornered."

"He has a machine gun, Ed."

"He's one man, Gary, for God's sake!"

Gary's wimpy questions thwarted any others and goaded the cops into their vehicles, all six local cars and the two state cars. Forming a ragged line, they made their way slowly across the parking lot. When they got to where the trees stood, sure enough, Mal's car sat by itself, one door open, the warning chime dinging.

The cops blabbed on the radio. "There's his car." "Looks like he abandoned it." "That's what it looks like." "What do you think, Tom?" Tom was the expert in the group, having served in Vietnam.

"I think we should proceed with caution. First of all, the car could be booby-trapped. Secondly, he could very easily be here, waiting, in the tree line. Thirdly, if he's on foot, he's armed and we have to let people in the vicinity of the mall know. We don't want him in somebody's house with a couple of kids as hostages."

"So what should we do, Tom?"

"Let's sit here for a minute."

As they were sitting, the mini-van from the news station rolled up behind them.

"What's that asshole TV crew doing? Somebody tell them to get out of here."

Phil, a state trooper, heaved himself out of his car and walked slowly back to the TV van. Phil said something about arrest if they didn't move. The frizzy reporter dared him to do his worst. The van stayed where it was.

The cameraman shot footage of the whole argument. Now the cops were not only sitting, they were videotaped sitting. Two more state vehicles arrived and they too pointed their headlights into the woods.

"I don't see any movement, Tom."

"I think some of us should go back and keep track of the fire."

"Yeah, you do that, Gary. You go back if that's what you want."

Tom made a decision. "If we proceed cautiously, we can commence a search of the area. Each car should act as a two-man team. One man stays back with his car, the other walks forward and inspects the area of woods in front of his vehicle for any indications as to the whereabouts of the suspect."

"Suspect? The guy killed six people."

"Who said that?"

"The staties say they're staying in their cars."

"They suck."

"Who said that?"

"It's not their friends who got killed."

"Shit, man, what's going on?"

"Let's just do this. C'mon. He's going to get away."

One cop emerged from each of the six vehicles, his pistol drawn. Hesitantly the men stepped in the direction of the woods. Using flashlights, they scoured what they could see, which wasn't much. Over the years, the few acres of woods had thickened into a dense tangle of brush and swamp maple.

"I don't see anything."

"The car is definitely empty. Should I check?"

"Don't touch the car!"

"Okay, the immediate area seems clear, now what do we do? Should we go deeper into the woods? Go up to the interstate?"

"No, that's dangerous, let's get back to the cars."

Each cop returned to his vehicle and the cops who had stayed inside their cars got out. They formed a knot of people, discussing the situation, keeping an eye on but not touching Mal's car. Someone arrived with fresh coffee and crullers. The state troopers finally joined them. Twenty men, plus the TV crew, stood around on the pavement of the shopping mall parking lot, lit only by one nearby vapor lamp and the headlights of the cars and the mini-cam. The suspect, they concluded, had left the area.

"He's probably gone by now. Long gone."

"Maybe, maybe not. If we stay here, he can't get out. We got him bottled up."

Although he couldn't hear Tom say the words, on *bottled up*, Mal began to rake the tight knot of relaxed men in short bursts. They formed a perfect target. Mal stood up near the ridge, the traffic of the interstate behind him and a clear line of fire over the thin treetops. He made three quick passes then moved off to another, closer spot in the middle of the trees to pick up the M-16. He did this four times, moving from one cache of ammo to the next.

Most of the men had fired their guns on a pistol range. But when the shooting started they forgot their weapons and ducked toward their respective cars. A few took cover and returned fire at what they thought was Mal's position, making themselves even better targets. He got bullets into most of them. The ones he didn't seriously wound or kill sped across the parking lot in their riddled cars. Once the able-bodied cops split, Mal emerged from the woods. Returning to his car he got out the remaining jugs of gasoline and, using his handgun, finished off the wounded and lit all the police cars on fire. The TV van was long gone. The driver had seen this coming, even though he had never served in Vietnam.

29

Danny pulled his face up off the carpet of wood chips. A few stuck onto his skin, but he didn't notice. The half pound of metal clamping his wrists was pouring liquid pain into his arms, into his head. He pulled himself up and sat, his arms locked behind him.

He thought of Carole Ann, the receptionist for a client in Chicago. She and Danny would joke whenever he came by the offices. He didn't think of her as beautiful, but he did think of her as sexy, her large bosom corseted by the tailored suits she'd wear. She wore more makeup than Judy, pouting her lips and making her dark eyes shine.

Carole Ann always had a smile for Danny. He was in the Chicago office at least once a week and found himself saying things like "How's my girlfriend today?" or "God, you look good enough to eat." Things he would never say if Judy were with him. Things he would never say at the home offices. Here it seemed acceptable, even appreciated. Chicago was different.

Once or twice, Carole Ann's boss got stuck in traffic and Danny was left alone with her for as long as an hour. He could have made phone calls or gone out for a walk, instead she made Danny coffee and together they enjoyed the warmth of the snug office. He showed her the snapshots in his wallet. Carole Ann loved the fact that Danny was so happily married, that he had kids, that he was a good dad. He told her she was obviously too smart for the job.

One day, Carole Ann's boss didn't show up at all. He was out with the flu and she hadn't had time to find Danny and tell him not to come in. They went to lunch together. Why not?

At lunch, Carole Ann's playfulness grew. When he made a joke about an ugly waitress, she tossed a breadstick at him. Everything Danny said was funny, as if he were the most charming man in the world. When the waiter came with their food (Danny had decided to splurge, so they went to one of his deductible haunts), they were so engrossed in their conversation they didn't even look up.

On the way out of the restaurant, as Danny got their coats from the coat check, Carole Ann laughed for no reason. When he handed her her coat, she looked him in the eye and touched his hand for a second. Danny glanced back, smiled tightly and, as if he were deciding on the fate of the free world, stated the fact: "My hotel is across the street, you know."

A fork in the road. Carole Ann had actually never been inside the hotel in all the years she'd passed it on the street. She'd always been curious about the place. Twenty minutes later, Carole Ann's curiosity was satisfied.

As Danny kissed and hugged Carole Ann, as he felt her breasts push into his chest, smelled her perfume, caressed the back of her neck, he felt like he was sipping from an exhilarating fountain of youth. He could sense the little hairs on his back stand up and his buttocks tighten. As his penis hardened, Danny was sure it had become larger than ever before. He was as excited as a little boy opening presents on Christmas morning. A little boy who had a huge hard-on, who was going to get to fuck a big, soft girl.

When Carole Ann pushed him onto his back and took him into her mouth, over her shoulder Danny could see the little bathroom a few feet away. There sat his shaving kit, his toothbrush, the crumpled tube of toothpaste he had snatched from the kids' bathroom only hours before. He saw Judy, the kids, his house, his life arrayed along the edge of the sink.

Once her clothes fell off, so did Carole Ann's familiar office persona, and she became a hungry voluptuous fantasy fuck. Danny loved that Carole Ann made more noise than Judy. She bounced more, spread her legs wider and stuck her tongue deeper into his mouth. Judy was always Judy, but Carole Ann was some kind of adult entertainment come to life. Danny, in turn, became a stud, lasting longer than he ever had in his hushed and roomy bedroom on Maidenbird Lane.

When Danny emerged from the shower, Carole Ann watched him cross the room, a stoned smile on her lips. He was a man again, tall and lean and full of juice. He met her eyes and, true to a mutually understood script, came to the bed, dropped his towel and entered her one more time.

As Danny boarded his first-class flight home, guilt flared like a brush fire. He was Don Juan, a connoisseur of the flesh, dallying over his new paramour. But he was also "Daddy" and "honey."

When Danny visited Chicago a month later, he cleared his schedule for his new mistress. He saw her every night for a week. On the last night, as Carole Ann lay snuggled in his postcoital arms, Danny found himself gazing contentedly upon her large bosom. Her breasts were full and round, her nipples a deep purple. In fact, Danny realized, she was sort of heavy.

Napping, she was turned in to him and a line had formed at her waist, a fold. A fold of fat. Like finding a tiny thread on the sleeve of a suit jacket, Danny couldn't resist pulling. He examined her more carefully, finding more imperfections. They were easy to find once he looked.

He could see the dye in her hair, her perfume was cheap, almost rank. Her skin wasn't blemish-free like Judy's but almost mottled in places. And she was short. Short and fat. As they made love once more, he stroked her body and felt repulsion.

As fast as the storm had blown in, it was over. The next time Danny came to Chicago, he made the excuse of a sore throat. The time after that, he arrived when she was out on an errand. In between times, he only called her when he knew she wouldn't be there. On his final visit, Danny discovered with relief and a different kind of guilt that Carole Ann no longer worked for his client.

Lying in the dark, his body battered and his heart pulsing dark blood, Danny felt Carole Ann's presence. Where was she? If he ever got out of this alive, he would find her and tell her he was sorry. He had known her in a way he shouldn't have. He had been her lover but really all he had been was a trespasser. He had tried to fix himself and instead he had been bad. And now he was being punished.

30

From Mal's vantage point in the woods, he could see the fallen figures arranged around the sputtering cop cars. Eventually this would get cleaned up. They would come, wary of another ambush, and Mal could begin the next phase of his plan. Forty-five minutes and the helicopters were finally arriving. This wasn't New York City, after all. The copter spotlights splayed over the mall's multilevel roofs ran across the lot, into the woods. Mal knew they couldn't see him. When they could, it would be too late for that too. Mal stubbed out his cigarette. Stood up and pissed on it. For the dogs. Because the dogs would be coming. Dogs and helicopters on a play date with Mal.

After the short rest, the speed in his system was building up a new head of steam. His cells cried out for activity. Time to get to work. First, Mal reloaded. With deft and practiced hand, he snapped fresh rounds into the flat plastic combat-style magazines, thirty rounds each rather than the ten. One by one he filled them as the copter passed by overhead, everything strobing white and then black again. In a kind of blindness, Mal worked.

This was an act of passion, each round representing an old scar, someone on his list. One by one the little brass-and-lead soldiers found their place. One for every teacher from second grade up through high school, each employer, each manager, each girlfriend, each aunt and uncle, each so-called friend. A bullet for each. If they weren't here to receive his gifts, Mal would give them to some other deserving soul. A twist on that old Stephen Stills song: "hate the one you're with." Mal finished his chores by checking the handguns, filling their reservoirs as well. He tightened the laces of his boots.

Mal stood and slung the M-16 over his shoulder. It took about fifteen minutes to make his way along the border of the woods, setting his traps. When he glanced out, he could see the bodies had been taken away. Two fire trucks had rolled over to where the cars burned and, seemingly unaware of the danger, the firemen sprayed foam on the hot metal. He heard a droning and checked his watch. Occasionally a fireman would look his way, but the firemen didn't want to see him, they wanted to keep moving, not sure if the maniac shot at firemen too.

Mal looked up and behind him. On the freeway the traffic had disappeared. Of course, the state troopers were diverting traffic from the last exit. Although Mal couldn't see them, he knew they were up there, on the ridge with night vision glasses and scope rifles, scanning the woods. They were so sure they had him. Out in the parking lot a fleet of station wagons arrived by the fire trucks and disgorged a half dozen Alsatians, grinning their doggy grins, circling, panting, drooling, finally heeling at their handlers' feet.

Mal shook out a Lucky and lit it. Then he opened the matches he had gotten from the fat girl with the big mouth and wrapped the cover around the stem of the lit cigarette. He placed the contraption onto a small pile of leaves and stepped away into the darkness. The dogs were snuffling and baying as the first one entered the woods. In twenty seconds, the cigarette would burn down to the heads of the paper matches and ignite the pack. "Ashes, ashes, we all fall down!"

31

Michel, unlike Mal, had no plan. He had heard the commotion as he made his way from the south end of the little woods. He stood in the dark and waited for something that would give him direction. As he stood motionless amongst the foliage, terror clotted the blood in his heart. He knew the dogs did not discriminate. They would find him as easily as they found the man with the gym bag. The dogs would smell his fear. Their wet, white teeth would come for him.

Michel squinted into the darkness in the direction he was heading, the neck of woods where he was certain the man was hiding. During the sniping, he had last seen flashes from that part and it was logical that the man was in there. But the dogs were in there too. If Michel stood his ground and waited, it was possible the man would get flushed down to where he stood and then Michel could shoot him with the shotgun.

Michel could not sort out the shadows. The interstate had grown very quiet and looking up Michel could see the troopers' cars edging the breakdown lane. The panting dogs were in the woods now. It was only a matter of time before they found someone. The man with the gym bag had two options: follow the strip of woods north or turn south, where Michel stood. Michel crouched down. Through the filigree of black branches, leaves and shadows, he saw the orange flames.

The fire moved so quickly, the dogs and their handlers became confused. Avoiding the flames they moved deeper into the woods, toward the ridge. A second line of fire was there, waiting for them, and by the time they got back the trees were impassable in places. One of the dogs yelped in fear. The fire trucks moved closer. Someone shouted a name.

Michel stayed where he was, waiting. The fire was moving toward him too. Then he sensed movement to his right, someone inching through the woods. Michel saw the slightest shadow, but what could he do? If he shot at it without calling out first, he might hit a policeman. If he called out first, he could be the target of the man with the machine gun, with no more protection than his one round. Michel did nothing.

Michel tried to follow the shadow, but it had moved past him now and behind him he heard what sounded like muffled explosions. Michel held tightly to the shotgun and moved southward through the woods, hoping he did not run into a statie and get mistaken for the man with the gym bag. He hoped no dogs found him. He hoped he did not get burned to death. And then he understood, what he had thought was fear was really a kind of happiness, an excitement. And Michel's step grew lighter.

32

"A disgruntled employee. That's what it said on the news." A man holding a beer stood by Donna's elbow. She had given in and joined the peanut gallery by the windows. Smoke, lit by the omnipresent mall lighting systems, billowed over the boxy building.

"Yeah? What about a disgruntled employee?"

"He shot some people and lit the place on fire."

"Oh. They said that on TV?"

"Yeah."

"How do they know that? Is the guy under arrest?"

For the first time, Donna's new friend looked at her. He was forty-something, with soft skin, brown eyes and a warm mouth.

"No, he's a fugitive."

"That's exciting. Maybe he'll come up here and we can buy him a drink." Donna held her buddy's gaze. He blinked.

"Yeah, I guess."

"That mall sucks. I hope it burns to the ground."

His smile said he hoped she was joking. "You do?"

"Don't you?"

"Me? I'm not from around here. I'm staying at the hotel next door. Had some business in the area, this is a good place to stay. I've never been in that mall, all the times I've stayed here. So I don't have an opinion."

"Really?" Donna wondered if this guy could be any stiffer. But boring people can be fun if you play them right. Donna feigned interest. "What kind of business?"

"I set up networks. LANs. You know? Computer stuff. New technology, so I have to supervise the setup. In another year or so, they won't need me. I'll become obsolete."

"That's nice." Donna adjusted her blouse over her breasts, brought her drink to her lips. "I'm a housewife."

"That's cool. Been doing some shopping?"

"Sort of. Just trying to unwind. You know?" Again Donna looked the soon-to-be-obsolete LAN technician in the eyes.

He glanced out the window, pretending that he and Donna were just guys watching the show, shooting the shit. "They've got every fire truck in the region down there."

Donna had no interest in fire trucks. "What's your name?"

"Len. Lenny. What's yours?"

"Donna."

Knowing Donna's name didn't make Lenny any more comfortable.

"Lenny. That's a nice name."

"My grandfather's name was Lenny. I was named after him."

"Really? So you're staying at the hotel? How is it?"

"It's good, it's good. You know how these places are. You been in one you been in them all." Lenny tried to look out the window. Donna touched his arm.

"Only time I've been in one was when we went to Orlando. To

visit Mickey, you know? Been to New Orleans once. That's about the extent of my exciting life of travel. But I go by here all the time. Driving my kids, carpooling, you know. Frustrated house-wife. I always think to myself, I wonder if those rooms are like the rooms in Orlando."

"Probably exactly the same."

"I'd love to see one."

"One what?"

"One of the rooms. Is there a mini-bar in your room?"

"Yeah."

"They have vodka?"

"I guess."

"Let's go check out your room."

Lenny avoided Donna's eyes. "I—"

"What? You'd rather stay here and watch the fire trucks?"

"No. I—"

"Lenny, come on! I just want to take a look at your room. One look! Did you leave your undies on the floor?"

"No, they clean them, I mean they clean the rooms every day."

"They do?" Donna wouldn't let Lenny's eyes go. He squirmed like a naughty boy. A win-win situation.

"Yeah."

Conspiratorially Donna asked, "New sheets?"

"Yeah."

"Then let's go."

Lenny searched for the waitress, anyone, to help him.

"Okay. Wait here a sec, I gotta hit the men's. Then we can go up. I guess. You sure about this?"

"Oh, yeah. Come right back. I'll keep an eye on the fire trucks for you."

Lenny slipped off toward the lobby where the rest rooms

were. Donna doubted she would see Lenny again tonight, so she reluctantly watched the fire trucks. She'd always had fantasies about firemen, bet they knew how to make a woman happy. Probably knew how to drink too. Probably knew about a lot of things.

33

Jeff wanted to cross the four-lane highway separating him from the brightly lit Jeep-Chrysler dealership across the way. He needed to get to those cars lined up so perfectly. He was hungry for order, the bright lights would banish the bad things.

Jeff eyed the traffic carefully, sussing out the ebb and flow. Normally negotiating crossing the street was easy, but right now Jeff couldn't remember how he did it. He found a gap in the pattern on his side and began to cross. As he did, the traffic in the transverse lanes grew thicker. He found himself stuck in the middle, cars whooshing past on both sides. Frenzy rippled through his limbs until he made it back to the safety of his starting point.

I'm using my primal mind and my primal mind cannot fathom traffic, he thought. Jeff looked to his right and saw the spot where he had been sitting only a few hours before. The spot where not so long ago he had conversed with the cop with the blond mustache. The dead cop.

An ambulance, maybe even carrying the cop's body, bounced up the ramp, sirens keening. Jeff saw himself watching the flashing van fly by and for a moment lost his place in the time-space continuum. Was he inside or outside the ambulance? Was he the cop with the blond mustache? Was he dead?

An insight came to him. He could walk up to the lights and cross there. So he did that.

As he made his way with ease across the roadway, Jeff marveled at the excellent invention called traffic signals. They were a simple system, on/off. One side flowed while the other side halted. One side was red while the other side was green. Two sides could not be red at the same time, nor could they both be green. It was either/or. Just like the binary code of computers. Just like life. You can't be in two places at the same time. You are either you or you are the other, but you can't be both.

Jeff didn't feel like he was completely someone yet, so he had to choose a direction to take. Life was made of endless choices and each choice closed doors and opened others, each sculpted who he was becoming. That didn't mean he didn't have an idea about who he wanted to be eventually, but he was wise enough to know that he couldn't predict the outcome from the actions he took right now. He was exploring. He was unformed. Was Adelle the future? Did he have a future? He was stuck, trying to cross the road of his destiny.

Others seemed more sure of who they were. They took a firm stand and acted from that position. Beckett knew who he was. Adelle knew who she was. Adelle was not the person Jeff thought she was. So it was okay that his love for her was unrequited. In fact, it was impossible to have unrequited love because you can't really love someone who doesn't love you. If they can't see who you are then that is a fault that prevents true love. Or something like that.

Jeff had made it across the road, but now he was stuck in front of the car dealership trying to puzzle out how a binary system related to passion. A paralysis was setting in. The lights here were ten times more intense than in the mall parking lot. They were blue-white and cast electric highlights on the shiny clones in their multicolored rows. The soft sizzle of the lamps filled the white air like invisible gnats.

Jeff's thoughts hiccuped. Maybe it was the drugs, but in a flash the knot in his mind was sliced in two. And he stood looking around, almost not sure how he got here. It was late, the dealership deserted. The salesmen were home having a beer and watching the final innings of the ball game. Tomorrow they would return for a new day of hustling, telling dirty jokes and exhaling Marlboro smoke out their nostrils.

Jeff worked his way through the parking lot. Tonight the police had their hands full and no one would notice him here. Jeff could hear more gunfire down by the mall. He shuddered.

The door handle of a blemish-free, metallic red LeBaron beckoned to Jeff. He lifted it, the mechanism unlatched with a happy click and the door swung open. What were the chances of finding an unlocked car? Jeff couldn't calculate it right now so he slid inside, sat and inhaled the warm plastic aroma. He had no key. He couldn't turn the radio on. He couldn't drive this car. But there was movement all around him. Is this my normal mind now, or is my normal mind the mind I have when I'm not tripping? The answer to that was obvious. But the obvious was not obvious right now.

What difference does it make if I think or I don't think? We're just these bags of flesh with sensors designed to make us think we're so precious. When you become disposable, your thoughts of your own preservation evaporate. I am disposable.

What if my mind went blank because I was in some hellacious car accident where all my limbs got cut off and I went blind but didn't know it? If I was still warm and fed, without a thought in my head, in a coma, someone would take care of me. I wouldn't know it, but I'd be alive. It wouldn't make any difference to the world and me. And I wouldn't care. It isn't like I have something to contribute and if something bad happened to me, anyone would miss me.

My life would come to a standstill. I'd be as unproductive as a stone and every day would be the same as the next. No progress, but what is progress? Buying a fleece vest? Getting more comfortable? Becoming a better skateboarder? Going to a bigger mall? It's all relative. Right?

And who says we've got it so good? Will people someday think of us and say, How could they have lived like that? It must have been barbaric? Will they think that? Is it? Was it? I can't imagine living in a nineteenth-century slum or crossing the great plains on a wagon train, but people did it. And they didn't complain that much. They didn't complain at all.

Jeff put his hands on the steering wheel. The thing felt like the collarbone of a strange and ugly beast.

In fact, those people thought people who lived a hundred years before them were incredibly barbaric and uncomfortable.

The truth is, and everyone knows it, that the thing we call civilization is what the Greeks invented two thousand years ago and since then it's never been as good. In fact, in most places on earth it's usually been worse. Today it's worse. Which is better, Red China or Ancient Greece? The slums of Rio or Ancient Greece? Westchester or Ancient Greece?

Jeff felt as if someone were watching him. He turned quickly. As he did, he elbowed the steering wheel, triggering an automotive bleat. If there was someone there, they were hiding now. The bright lights and lack of shadows made its own kind of ghosts. The false daylight was spooky.

Jeff was feeling restricted and hot, trapped inside the LeBaron.

The colors irritated him. In a panic, he grabbed at the door handle and, after a couple of tries, got it open and fumbled out into the light. His feet found the trustworthy pavement. Jeff's mouth was tacky and parched. The blinking lights of the Ramada Inn beckoned.

34

Danny stayed in the bushes long enough to realize the chorus of sirens had nothing to do with him. Something was happening besides his Peeping Tom episode, even beyond the dead cop. Flashes of color outlined the new low clouds perched on top of the mall. The guy who had shot the cop and doused the police car had done something else as well. Maybe shot other people, started other fires. Danny could hear vehicles racing back and forth, although from his spot in the foliage he couldn't see much.

Danny tried to bring his cuffed wrists below his heels so that he could at least hold his hands in front of him, but that only worked in movies. Danny had his car keys on him. His car was still somewhere in the lot, but everything was turned around, he couldn't remember where. He'd wait a little longer and then find his car, and somehow, he would drive his car home. Is it possible to turn a steering wheel with your teeth?

He heard a dog snuffling around the foundation of the building. How would a dog get here? How could it cross the parking lot? Then he heard the voices.

"C'mon, under here, man, they won't see us here."

When they saw Danny they weren't sure how to react. Was he some kind of weird suburban homeless person? Then they understood, he was the guy from the cop car. Danny knew who they were immediately.

"Hey, it's the pervert. The pervert is in here hiding."

"You're the guy. Did you escape?"

Danny's throat burned. His arms hurt, he could feel where his back had been scorched. His eyes were gummy.

"I think he's in shock, man."

"Are you in shock, dude?"

Beckett and Terry moved closer to Danny, checking him out.

"Dude, he's still got handcuffs on. And he's charred up!"

"Yo, you idiot, he was in the police car that got burnt to shit."

"Man, are you all right?"

Danny managed one syllable: "No."

"You're not?"

"No. I'm not. Why don't you help me?"

"Why should we help you?"

Terry reached out toward Danny. "Let me see the handcuffs?" Danny turned and showed Terry his bound wrists.

"Does this hurt?" Terry pulled upward and Danny lurched forward, his face lunging into the ground.

Beckett shoved Terry aside. "Hey, man. Don't do that."

Shel moved closer to Danny. "This is the guy who was looking in the dressing rooms. He likes to look at pussy. You like to look at pussy?"

Danny tried to hop up onto his feet, but Terry grabbed his sleeve. Shel continued the interrogation. "You want to look at my pussy?"

"I just want to go home."

Automatic gunfire rattled in the distance, sounding almost natural in the dreamy nightscape.

"Where's the cop who arrested you?"

"He's dead. Someone shot him."

"Wow. It's like that thing that happened in California."

Adelle appeared, pushing through the shrubbery. "Where'd you guys go?"

"You were talking to Jeff? Where's Jeff?"

"He freaked out."

"I hope he doesn't go near the woods. That's where the lunatic is."

Danny found more words: "I saw him, the lunatic."

"You saw him?"

"Please help me with these."

"What did he look like?"

Danny bartered words for aid. "Crazed. Nuts."

Terry picked up the word like a toy. "Crazed. Oh yeah! The 'crazed gunman.' There is a crazed gunman situation here tonight. He lit the mall on fire, killed some cops. More at eleven!"

"There's shooting over in the woods. It's on TV. 'The whole world is watching!'"

Danny feigned interest. "Please."

Adelle gently touched the handcuffs. "These must hurt."

"They do." Danny sought her kind face.

Adelle looked into Danny's eyes. "Everything's going to be okay."

Danny smiled up at her, a savior at last.

35

Dry leaves crackling, Michel brought each heavy foot down with care as he moved through the woods. Alert, eyes dilated, straining to see in the darkness, muscles tensed, ready. The acid aroma of the leaves mixed with the smell of the night. He knew two things: the woods were surrounded by police and his quarry was somewhere in front of him. If he left the woods, a black man carrying a shotgun, the police would shoot him. The dogs would chase him. He would end his time in the United States hunted, maybe dead.

Making a choice, even a bad one, made Michel feel in control. An opportunity arose and opened like a gate through which a man could step. This was such an opportunity.

The fire engines sprayed plumes onto the small trees. Smolder took the place of flame. The dogs that had escaped barked plaintively, smelling the burned fur of their cousins. The skinny man had taught man and beast a lesson. The men in uniform would proceed with extreme caution from now on. Michel continued along stealthily, fairly sure no one would be entering the woods anytime soon.

He adjusted his eyes to the filtered light. Although it was dark here, the mall and the highway above gave off so much luminescence, Michel could almost see. A dog barked behind him, but he could not tell if the dog was coming closer or going away. The fire had confused the dogs. Michel knew this. He listened again. Contained in the noise of sirens and men shouting back in the parking lot, Michel heard a small metallic sound in the trees before him. He inched forward and pressed up against a sapling, concentrating his vision on the area. He heard the clicking again and adjusted the angle of his vision slightly. He saw movement. There, crouched down, was the skinny man, nothing more than a cutout of the darkness amongst shadows.

Michel knew what the man was doing. He was refilling clips, reloading for the next firefight. The man had numerous weapons, plenty of ammo. Michel only had one shell. If Michel did not hit him, he would get fired upon and he would get hit.

Michel took a careful step forward and then, to steady his aim, went down on one knee. Slowly, like blackstrap molasses down a bottleneck, Michel brought the shotgun up to his shoulder and sighted. Firing a shotgun at a stationary target not twenty feet away was not difficult. Michel's heart thundered and his vision blurred.

The man reached back and grabbed something out of his bag. As he did, his position relative to the gun barrel changed and a sapling crossed the line extending from the end of the muzzle to the center of the man's forehead. Michel aimed at the naked part where there could be no body armor, no Kevlar vest.

Michel readjusted, standing very slowly, stepping forward and dipping down into a crouch once more. But as he put his bent right leg forward, steadying his shooting arm on his knee, his entire center of gravity shifted, all two hundred and fifty pounds. Michel was somersaulting into space.

He was so surprised he almost yelped. In the dark he had not seen the minuscule stream in its concrete culvert running along the lower edge of the incline. Michel had placed his foot forward onto nothing.

The thudding scrabble and crunch entered Mal's bristling nervous system. He rapidly rolled down and away, spraying the spot where Michel had begun to squat, shattering the skinny trees and digging up the soil. But Michel was no longer where he had been, he had fallen into the ditch, below Mal's line of sight.

As the gunfire traced above him, Michel twisted in the sodden oak leaves and puddles lining the bottom of the concrete channel. He grabbed for his shotgun, keeping low, feeling the whizzing overhead. In the following stillness, he froze, immobile. The trickling stream flowing over the hard bottom soaked into the heavy cloth of his pants. He was vulnerable. If the man knew where he was, it would be no trouble at all to stand over him and hammer him with a fusillade.

On the other hand, Michel was in a trench and if the man peered over the edge for a second he too would be a perfect target.

As Michel waited, chest throbbing, Mal had already begun his exit. He wasn't sure if he had shot his visitor or if there was an intruder at all, but he was not waiting around to find out. His mind flashed back: Cover area with automatic fire, move. Wait, listen. As still and alert as a cat, hearing no more sound, Mal grabbed the bag and the automatic rifle and scuttled upward, toward the highway.

• • •

This is a grave, thought Michel. I can lie here all night or I can move. If I move, maybe I die. Maybe not. If I don't move, they may as well cover me with dirt.

Michel clambered up out of the trench noisily, a mistake. One shot whizzing over his shoulder answered him from deep in the woods. Firing in that direction would be a waste. He had only one shell, now was not the time. Behind him he could hear the dogs barking. He had no choice but to follow Mal up the incline, toward the highway.

36

Beckett examined Danny's handcuffs. He marveled at their construction.

"This is interesting. Think about it: If we don't help you get these off and if you never find the key, you could never get free. Like if you were on a desert island, you'd starve."

Terry nodded thoughtfully. "You'd have to cut one hand off."

Beckett didn't look up. "If you cut the hand off you'd bleed to death."

"Not me, him."

Beckett fondled the cuffs, the reddened wrist. "This is what it was like for the slaves, man."

"What slaves?"

"The slaves in the slave boats. Chained together. Sometimes they'd die and they wouldn't set 'em free until they hit port."

"I saw a movie about it. Sometimes they were just thrown overboard."

"Handcuffs are a modern invention. Perfect in every way. You know how in James Bond movies they can like pick the lock? You could never pick this lock." Beckett looked around as if waiting for someone to dare challenge him.

Shel watched Beckett's eyes. "Are you still tripping, Beckett?"

Beckett looked up and felt Adelle's eyes on him. "I'm not sure. Maybe."

Danny observed their pale young faces. They were what? At least fifteen years younger than him? Their eyes are dark. Very dark. They probably play video games for days. "Listen, you guys got a car?" He tried to put a casual lilt in his voice. He needed them to like him.

Terry was affronted by the question. "No."

Danny craned his neck to address Terry. Was he the leader? "Well, I do. Why don't we go find my car and you can drive me somewhere and we can break the handcuffs off my wrists. I'll pay you."

Shel's eyes danced and she laughed. "Oh man, this guy is so desperate."

"Of course I'm desperate."

"Why don't we just give you back to the police, you pervert?"

Danny tried to face Shel. "I'm not a pervert. I didn't do anything wrong. They made a mistake."

"That's what they all say."

Beckett pulled himself up out of his reverie. "Where's your car?"

"I don't know, it's a Saab."

"Terry, go scout around the parking lot and find a Saab, then come back and tell us where it is. Where's your keys?"

Danny's heart lifted. This guy is the leader. "In my pocket."

Beckett smiled benevolently at Danny and patted his shoulder.

"Okay, find the car, then we'll go over and drive it back here and we'll sneak him in."

Beckett glanced at Adelle. She smiled back. Danny thought, She's into me. That's what this is about. Be nice to her and she'll follow.

37

On the incline Mal propped himself against a tree, his breath coming in hard little sucks. He wondered what was in the woods with him. That someone had joined him intrigued Mal. Ten people were already gone from this earth. Whatever happened now, no matter if they dropped a nuclear bomb on him, they couldn't undo what he had done.

If he could hang in there, he could have more fun. If they shot and killed him, it would be over. If they somehow captured him alive, which Mal knew probably wouldn't happen, he would be a "guest of the state" for a long time, with all kinds of amusing trials and interviews and things to do. He was sure he'd love giving those interviews. Every time he saw Charlie Manson on TV, the guy looked pretty happy.

Mal steadied his breathing. He tried to see into the woods behind him. Nothing. No movement. No unusual shapes. Squatting on the wooded incline leading up to the interstate, he could hear the chatter of the troopers' radios "cutting him off" above. Back where the fires were being extinguished, he could hear shouts and curses threading the night air. When he looked up into the night sky, Mal counted two more helicopters hanging above, adding their dull buzzsaw drone to the symphony. Good.

The smoke would screw up the dogs' snouts, at least for tonight. The sun wouldn't be up for at least six more hours. Mal was in a place where no one would think to look. Besides, what idiot would enter these woods now? As long as he didn't move, no one could find him. Not even his new friend. Mal let his back skid down the smooth skin of the maple sapling until his butt touched the ground. He tilted his head back against the bark and fell into a deep pseudosleep. Fizzy black blankets of exhaustion layered over him. He hung onto one idea: he was alive. He was sure of that. He was alive and kickin'. *Yee-haw,* he hollered deep inside his head.

38

Jeff entered the dark brown foyer of the lounge, another dimension. Before him was a moody grotto of brown wood and tinted glass, red and mellow yellow lighting luring him deeper into the belly of the bar. The steady thrum of the traffic, the flashing police lights, the grind of fire vehicles wove the background tapestry.

This wasn't the sort of hangout Jeff ever visited with his friends. It reminded him of his father and mother before they got divorced, when the whole family would go out for a Sunday drive and end up having a late lunch at a place like this. His dad would order the steak medium rare and get Thousand Island dressing on his salad. His mother would always order the fish, as if by eating fish rather than meat she would improve herself in some way. She was always improving herself, but Jeff never noticed any change. Jeff and his sister would fight over the crackers and bread.

Jeff pondered how many places there might be just like this one all over the country. Millions? Billions? How many steaks, fried potatoes, grim little salads topped with cherry tomatoes?

Cherry tomatoes were a foodstuff Jeff never ate at home, but they were part of virtually every salad he ever ate outside of it. So that would mean, logically, that somewhere vast cherry tomato farms pumped out these fruits for the zillions of salad bars across the U.S. Probably in some third-world country where they were picked by people getting paid five cents an hour. People who lived lives of quiet desperation, who spoke some variation of Spanish and tried to feed their dark, round-faced children as best they could while solemn men gripping American-made automatic weapons stood sentinel over them.

That was the way of the world. The world was cruel and always had been. Then Jeff had a huge realization, one that had eluded him in the midst of all his tortuous thoughts—the world was *not* cruel to him. Since the only thing he really knew was his own experience, any notion of a cruel world was merely conceptual. Maybe it was a mirage, something concocted by the media to frighten everyone into toeing the line. Jeff wanted to shout, "Eureka!"

Then he remembered Adelle and his chest went hollow. Adelle with her perfect skin and cool eyes had been cruel to him. He was unhappy about that. So unhappiness, maybe not the third-world kind, rather the first-world kind, was definitely in his life. He couldn't think himself out of it. It didn't make any difference why you felt bad. If you felt bad, you felt bad.

Perplexed, Jeff stood in the musty entranceway of the lounge. Actually he couldn't figure out if he was happy or sad. In a way, the "breakup" with Adelle was a relief because now he didn't have to test himself by chasing her around anymore. He was free. And freedom was a good thing.

A young woman in a black skirt and white apron was talking to him. She had stepped right out of his own recollected dinners with his family. She was the ur-waitress. Jeff marveled at her friendliness. She was looking straight at him and asking him something.

"Are you eating?"

Are you eating? What could she mean by that? She could see he was not eating.

"Uh, what?"

"Are you eating? Or just drinking?"

"I'm thirsty."

"Well, we're not too busy, so you can sit at a table if you want. I'll be right over."

Jeff drifted toward one of the tables, but the sight of the middle-aged couples fiddling with their meals nudged him toward the bar. There the multicolored neon beer signs swarmed and wriggled. Behind them the bottles and mirrors blended into a palette of brown and pale orange. All this made him feel better.

"Yeah?"

One syllable was all the bartender was going to expend on him. Jeff could feel the distrust. Maybe the bartender was an off-duty cop, always on the alert for teenagers on drugs? Maybe Jeff was being sized up? Jeff couldn't process the parameters. He stared hard at the glib, beefy guy behind the bar.

"What can I get you, kid?"

No, he was just a bartender. "Heineken?"

With a looping move, a crack and a hiss, a green bottle and a clean glass appeared before Jeff. Jeff sipped and the cold bitter fluid ran down his throat and straight into his veins. Jeff was flooded with happiness. Any bad thoughts were swept away by the goodness of beer and glass bottles and reliable bartenders.

"You come from the mall?"

The bartender was speaking again.

"The mall?"

"Yeah, you been over there? What's happening?"

"A fire. Some shooting. I think someone's been killed."

As if Jeff were doing no more than citing a baseball statistic, the bartender raised his eyebrows. "Yeah?"

"Yeah." Jeff tried to mimic the bartender's nonchalance. The guy looked much less like a cop now, more like a kindly uncle. The bartender turned to the waitress as she sailed past. "This kid says someone got shot over there."

"Yeah, that's what I heard."

"Shit. I hope it isn't anybody I know."

"Well, it's somebody. You can bet on that. And that's bad enough."

"True enough. True fucking enough."

As the waitress tossed a fresh drink order at the barkeep, Jeff swallowed another mouthful of beer. The coolness ran out of the core of his torso into his limbs, into his fingers and toes. He wondered if he could be drunk and tripping at the same time. As he worked on this calculus, Donna returned to her place at the bar, Lenny the LAN salesman nothing more than a short-term memory.

One empty bar stool stood between Donna and Jeff.

"Someone got shot over there?"

Jeff turned and noticed Donna for the first time. He shaped his words carefully.

"I saw a body on a stretcher. I think he got shot."

"I was just over there shopping. What part of the mall?"

"Penney's."

"Penney's?"

"Yeah. A tuxedo store is on fire. There are a lot of fire trucks."

Donna watched Jeff's lips move. They moved in lovely round shapes. Blue eyes, clear. Clear and pretty.

"Wow. You saw the bodies, huh?"

"Yeah."

"What did you do to your hair?"

"Dreads. If you don't comb your hair, it does that after a while."

"Oh." Donna wondered what his hair smelled like.

"It's too bad. 'Cause you know, if you weren't wearing rags and your hair didn't look like dried seaweed, you'd be kind of cute."

"Yeah, well, sorry to disappoint you."

"You're not disappointing me. In fact, I think you've got guts making yourself look so weird. What's your name?"

"Jeff. Uh. What's yours?"

"Donna."

The bartender repeated the drinks. The roomful of people chewing on their steaks and buttering their hot rolls became background noise, then evaporated. Jeff wasn't sure how he got here, but he was sitting at a bar talking to a strange woman named Donna.

"How come you're sitting here at the bar by yourself?" Jeff asked.

Donna took a second to construct an answer. "People suck out loud. I hate people."

"Especially when there's a lot of them."

Donna smiled wistfully. "Oh, I hate them individually too."

Jeff didn't want to go there. "Hate's a strong word. I don't like . . . I don't like bad things happening to people. No matter who they are."

"Are you all right? Your eyes look a little watery."

"Yeah, I'm fine. Just kickin' back, you know?" Jeff had stopped smiling.

"You like to kick back? You look pretty serious to me."

"No, I do. I . . ." Jeff smiled.

"Oh, he *smiles!* I like to kick back too. Let's kick back together."

"I thought you didn't like people."

"You're not people, you're Jeff. Hi, Jeff!"

Jeff turned and let himself look at Donna for the first time. She smiled and he fell into her eyes. He hadn't noticed when she first started talking to him, but she was beautiful in a way, her skin soft and faintly radiant, her eyes deep and large and her lips full. Jeff wondered how he'd describe her if he were writing all this down. He wondered if he was attracted to her. He thought maybe he was.

39

His head back, his arms locked over his knees, Mal was as rigid as porcelain. His nervous system had curled into itself, letting his limbs rest and recuperate. He was collecting his energies, absorbing every sound, every murmur around him in the woods.

A hot breeze grazed his cheek and his mind drifted. He sized up his situation. He was one hundred and seventy-five pounds of human organism. But he was not cooperating with the big bullshit game. He was not one more worker bee, he was not obeying the rules. He was breaking the rules. He was causing havoc. He was killing. When the big guys did it—the companies and the governments—nobody gave a shit. Only the little guys weren't allowed to kill. Big rule. Big rule.

Mal let the words *big rule* float in his simmering brain jelly. His exhaustion did not allow an idea to remain coherent for more than a minute before dissolving like sugar in hot coffee. His body was desperately trying to put itself back together, digest the cookies and cream, rest, think. But it couldn't because the crystal meth kept his sack of innards in a permanent state of fight or flight. He was redlining as intensely as a weasel caught in a trap.

This was nothing new for Mal. His thinned hair was colorless, his teeth were loose, boils and scabs peppered his flesh. But he was still alive. Because he knew how to pace himself. He had a tremendous urge to leap up, open his eyes and run through the woods screaming, firing hot streams of bullets. But this was art, to pace himself and wend his way through this suburban watering hole, killing, burning, scaring the piss out of everybody.

Mal had spent years doing nothing, taking up space. As far as he was concerned that's what everyone else did as well. No one wanted to admit it. Like dumb dinosaurs caught in a pool of tar, everyone pretended that it was all okay, until it was too late. When they ended up on a hospital bed in a bad-smelling, semi-private room, surrounded by pathetic friends and family and self-ish children, everyone eventually realized how pointless the whole thing had been. How all the shopping, holiday get-togethers, school exams, job promotions, traffic jams, TV specials, distant wars and sexual games had been for *nada*.

Mal, despite his failure as tuxedo store employee, rack-jobber and son, was really alive, right now. To be alive for three hours was more than most people got. And he was injecting his life into the hearts and souls and blood of all these good folk trying to stop him. They should be grateful, he thought. They're all walking in their sleep and I'm the alarm. Not soft muzak like Ma likes on the clock radio in the morning, but the buzzer that yanks a fucker into hyperventilation, gets his heart thumping hard and straightens his ass right out.

Mal conserved his strength, let his stomach try to do its work, tried to repair his ravished brain cells. His mind's eye floated in and out of a kind of coma, alternating between flat black nothingness and nightmares of wandering over gray deserts, lunar landscapes in hell. Under his crooked legs lay the guns. Beside him sat the gym bag with the ammunition. He felt good. And there was nothing better than that.

40

One hundred feet from where Mal hibernated, Michel waited, breathing softly. He intuited Mal had stopped moving. It was possible that Mal had run to another part of the woods, but Michel had figured out by now that Mal was smart and the best thing to do was to wait him out. Michel didn't mind waiting. The dampness in his clothes cooled him and for the first time tonight he could rest his swollen feet. He lay on his back, looking up at the stars. By his right arm lay the shotgun with one last tube of shot and powder. Unless the dogs came again, he was safe. No one could see him. He would wait. Recoup.

Michel thought of the stars as eyes of saints floating above, guarding him. Perhaps one of them was Marie. He missed her so badly. He didn't know what to do with himself when she wasn't there. He couldn't watch TV because it all looked the same to him, either people laughing at unfunny situations or bloody violence. But he had no interest in the wars, he had seen enough in Haiti. And the wrestling and ultimate fighting shows bored him. So he daydreamed.

When Michel was small, he had a uniform and a primer in French that contained all his lessons. His uncle had bought him a pencil box and he prized it. He would tie a faded blue strap around the pencil box and the primer and with one hand sling the parcel over his shoulder. With his other he carried a battered English biscuit tin holding two pieces of bread spread with some bacon drippings, wrapped in a sheet of newspaper. On the many days when the weather was fine, the walk to school was calm and sweet.

Of course, when Michel was a boy, he took all this for granted. But now, as a man, he returned to that schoolhouse walk. It pleased him to recall the warm sun on his shirtback, the feeling of the dust and pebbles under his bare feet and the weight of the book strap pressing into his shoulder. The road was dry and predictable, the tropical greenery punctuated every hundred feet with a shack of gaily painted tin and cinderblock. Scabby mutts would lie on their side in the yards. Friends and aunties would wave at him as he made his way to school.

He tried to recall every detail. Some parts were easy—the brush jungle trying to strangle the pitted road, the cane fields, the drool of the tethered old mule, the yellow dogs lying on the hot dirt. Some parts were simply inventories—the name and face of every person he passed. Some were sensual—the warm sun, the crackle of morning cooking, muffled laughter. He heard again the cooing of the wild pigeons.

The hardest to recall were the smells. There were many, from the smell of rain on the ochre dust to the aroma of frying plantains from an open-air kitchen. One day, Michel found a large dead snake stretched across the road. It had been flattened by truck tires and its light green body was dotted where the purple-red innards had squished out between the ribs of its skin. This smell was new to Michel, not only the smell of decayed meat, but a rotting vegetal smell, as if the greenness of its body was spoiled as well. By the next day, the carcass was gone.

Michel knew all about snakes. He knew them from chance encounters under the boards of his mother's house and from stepping on them in the brush. He knew the snakes that came down from the trees, called down by the voodoo priests, the proxies of Dambala, the staff of Moses. He knew the power snakes had to change a life.

On this night, as Michel lay on the dry leaf mulch of this miniature forest, he gathered up the smells and inventoried them. He could smell the leaves, and he could smell the doused fire. He could smell the young maples and he could even smell the asphalt of the parking lot fifty yards away. He could smell the exhaust and gasoline from the interstate above, could smell the humidity and he could smell himself. Usually, he liked his own smell, even at the end of the day, but tonight his body odor was masked with the stink of fear and it entered his nostrils sour and nasty.

Michel could smell the oil and burned powder of the shotgun lying next to him. He could smell the wetness of his clothing. He could smell the charred green wood lingering in the air. He focused and pulled in millions of molecules and he smelled one more thing—a man. This was a different odor than his, pungent and angry. The air settled and stilled all around him. Michel let the man's festering stink direct him.

41

Jeff and Donna took a cozy table by the window where they could watch the comings and goings of emergency personnel across the roadway. He drank beer and she sipped her vodkas. Outside in the world, chaos reigned, people struggled, death was dealt. In the lounge, the air conditioning kept the atmosphere temperate and silken. The little bowls of goldfish crackers nourished. The alcohol cleared the path.

Jeff brimmed with good cheer. The wood grain of the table was smooth and worn, the muzak strangely invigorating, the little goldfish sparkled and swam circles in their tiny sea. The anxiety that had signaled the onset of Beckett's drug was shifting into a smoother flux of good vibrations. On top of it all, a very, very pleasant, very pretty woman was sitting across from him, smiling at him.

Before this Jeff had never fantasized about older women. Now he allowed himself the pleasure of imagining this mature, buxom woman naked in his arms. Of course, he knew she was out of his league, he was a scruffy guy not even in college yet.

But he also knew he was young and he took a shower every morning and that he was a good kisser.

"So what are you, a student?"

Jeff lied. "College."

Donna saw the lie in his eyes. "Uh-huh. What are you studying?"

"Literature."

"Really? Books?"

"Uh-huh."

"What's your favorite book?"

"Right now it's *Steppenwolf.*"

"Steppenwolf? The band?"

"No, it's by, you know, the guy who wrote . . . never mind. Uh . . . what's your favorite book?"

"I pretty much stick to movies, stuff like that. But you know what I liked a lot? That one about the vampires down in New Orleans." Donna liked Jeff. He talked, he asked questions, he wasn't two jumps ahead of the game. Sweet.

"Anne Rice." Jeff had never read Anne Rice, but he knew who she was.

"Yeah. They made a movie with Tom Cruise. But I liked the book better. I even got . . . this friend of mine to take me to New Orleans."

"Did you like New Orleans?" Jeff felt like a talk show host.

"Yeah. It's a sexy place, you know? Hot. Everybody's in a great mood all the time. They know how to live down on Bourbon Street. You ever been there? Or out by the old mansions? There are these trees with stuff hanging off of them."

"Sphagnum moss."

"Moss. Yeah! When did you go there?" Donna's eyes sparkled with interest.

"I never been. I read about it."

"I felt good the whole time I was there. I bought a little cloth voodoo doll at Marie Laveau's. All black with pins. When I don't like somebody, out come my pins!"

"I better watch out."

"You better! What's your favorite place?"

"I want to travel, but I haven't had the time."

"Well, if you could go anywhere, where would you go?"

"Vienna."

"Wow, Vienna. Like the coffee? Why in the world would you want to go there?"

"Beethoven and Freud hung there. I figure if I went there I would feel the history."

"I like that. 'Feel the history.' That's cool. No one I know would ever say something like that. My . . . friend . . . would never say that. You're like an intellectual, right?"

"Who's your 'friend'?"

"My husband. I'm married. See?" Donna flashed her ring.

"Oh."

Jeff gave a sideways glance out the window as if Donna's husband were about to materialize right there in the parking lot.

"He's not here. He's at home. With my kid. I've got a kid. I shouldn't even be here right now, you know?"

"You don't look old enough to have a kid."

"I'm not that old. I mean, you're looking at me like I'm old."

"I didn't say you were old."

"Yes, you did."

"You're not much older than I am."

"What do you know? Maybe I'm younger than you are."

"Maybe."

"Do you think I'm attractive?"

"That's a weird question."

"Do you?"

"Yeah. More than that."

"Than what?"

"Attractive."

"What's more than attractive?"

"You know."

"What? Tell me." Donna was liking him more and more.

"You know what you are. Whoa." Jeff steadied himself against the table.

"What? Are you okay?"

"Yeah, I don't think I should have any more beer."

"You wanna get some fresh air?" Donna was already tugging him up from his chair.

"Yeah. Maybe that would be a good idea."

In a kaleidoscopic flurry of movement Jeff flashed past tables and people and the lobby, past the diamond-shaped panes of glass in the dark brown wood doors and past the rubber mat and back out into the parking lot. Then, from a blur, everything—colors, sounds, shapes, his skin—snapped back into sharp focus. No edges, then edges. Donna stood next to him, lighting a cigarette. The warm air massaged him, hugged him. She put one hand on his arm.

Donna's face popped out at him. "This is better out here, isn't it?"

"Yeah, I don't know what that was."

"You're a cheap drunk."

"Well, no, 'cause I, I had something to drink before."

"Oh. Me too. Where's your car?"

"I don't have a car. I hitched up here."

"Wow. Those were the days. Tell me the truth, you're not a college student." Donna was liking him more every minute.

"Yes, I am."

For a few moments Donna and Jeff said nothing. The dampened fire and the fire trucks across the way flickered in their pupils.

"I wonder how it's going down there."

"It was a cop. One of the people who got shot. I had talked to him a few hours ago. I got freaked when I saw him lying there. I never saw a dead person before." Jeff heard his own voice saying the words.

"Are you sure he was dead?"

"Oh yeah, he was dead." His voice was moving farther and farther away.

Stepping on her cigarette butt, Donna brightened up. "I have an idea! Let's sit in my car and listen to the radio and see what's happening."

With another blur of movement, Jeff found himself sitting in Donna's detailed Lincoln as she fiddled with the radio. This car didn't smell new like the LeBaron in the dealer's parking lot. It smelled like leather and tobacco.

"This is a big car."

"It's not mine. It's Roy's. He's so anal about it he leaves it home and takes my piece of shit Mazda. It's nice but I have to be careful. He'd have a heart attack if I left a soda can on the floor, let alone nick a bumper. See, my husband is into big cars. You know what they say: big car, small dick."

"Is it true? Does your husband have a small dick?"

"That's private. But no, he doesn't. He has a regular old dick. Just the right size. Unfortunately, he doesn't know how to use it."

"Oh."

"I can't find anything but ads. What kind of music do you like? You like country?"

The car was suddenly flooded with country harmony, a gal wailing about how she was a "happy girl."

Jeff could feel the music closing in on him. "It's like you're in-side the sound."

"Nice, huh? One of the good things about this car."

"Yeah. But could you turn it down a bit?" The anxiety was re-turning.

Donna obliged Jeff, turned and faced him. "Wow. This is weird, huh? I don't even know you and we're parking in this car together. Are you thinking what I'm thinking?"

"You want me to read your mind?" Jeff wondered if he could.

"Yeah. Read my mind, can you do that?"

Jeff gazed into Donna's black pupils. Her scent permeated everything, inhabiting him. In the dusk of the car she had be-come even more beautiful. A siren wailed in the distance. A car door slammed.

Neither one spoke. Jeff shifted his weight and moved an inch or two closer to Donna. Donna, behind the wheel, turned her whole body toward him. Jeff felt his chest shivering. "Should I guess?"

"Yeah. Take a big guess."

Jeff laughed.

Donna smiled at him, tilting her head slightly.

"What?"

"I had a crazy idea," Jeff said crazily.

"What?" Donna mimicked his smile.

"I had the idea that I could kiss you."

"Wow, what a crazy idea! Where'd you get that idea?"

Jeff felt his pulse explode, could feel his dick stiffen in his jeans. As high as he was, he ascended.

"I could."

"Could you? You sure?" Donna wanted to hug him, he was be-ing so adorable!

Jeff cast all caution to the wind, leaned forward and, like a dam breaking, kissed Donna. To his surprise, she kissed him back, her tongue touching his.

Unsure of the next step, Jeff put a hand on her upper arm, feeling that somehow this couldn't be of her free will. But Donna simply lifted his hand and pushed it onto her breast, like a mother might urge a nursing baby.

Jeff could taste the bitter liquor and cigarettes. Donna could feel his skinny, hard body and the tight spot in his jeans. They did this, kissing and groping and struggling, making twisted shapes on the ample front seat of the luxury car, until they broke apart like wrestlers looking for a new hold.

The horny appetite, which had brought every hair on Jeff's head to attention, competed with the woozy feeling suffusing his limbs, a combination of love and drugs. Donna, on the other hand, had a sense of survival.

"We can't do this," she said.

"We're doing it."

"Jeff. What a nice name—Jeff. Goofy but nice. No, Jeff, we're in the middle of a parking lot. The people in the bar, everyone, saw us meet up. We're in the middle of the parking lot making out."

"Yeah, isn't it great?"

Without another word, Donna popped her door and, grabbing her bag, got out of the car. Before closing the door she turned to Jeff and tossed her cell phone at him.

"Wait here. I'll call you in five minutes."

Jeff took the phone and examined it like he'd never seen one before in his life. When he looked up, Donna was gone.

42

Danny sat scrunched in the backseat of his Saab while Terry wrenched the stick shift and chewed up the transmission. In rocking spasms, they made it up the ramp of the mall and down the road toward the Burger King. Shel, in the shotgun seat, sulked. "This guy's a fugitive. We should just turn him over."

Beckett put his arm around Danny. "Guys, c'mon, the guy needs our help. Let's figure out how to get the cuffs off. You know where we could find a blowtorch?"

Terry caught the last wink of yellow as the light turned red. An airhorn blasted the Saab. As he spun the wheel, he turned and grinned at Danny. "We could kill him right now, stick him in the woods and no one would ever know it was us."

Beckett kept an eye on the truck bearing down on their rear. "We'd know."

Danny's thoughts roiled and churned. He didn't know these young people at all. They were capable of anything, why should he trust them? They could kill him. They could cut him to pieces and leave the bagged chunks by some highway rest stop.

Danny imagined the mourners at his wake. His stooped father trying to avoid people's curious glances, the last thoughts of his son shameful and rancid. His sister smirking with the I told you so's. And his mother. He couldn't imagine his mother in this situation. Every time he tried to conjure her face, he only came up with a smudge.

Judy would be grief-stricken. Unconsolable. But Danny had read somewhere that sixty percent of widows usually find someone else. Even if she thought she wouldn't, she would. She would remarry and probably have an outrageously satisfying sex life with the next guy. Danny could hear her moans: "Oh yeah, oh God, my late husband was never this good!" He could see her mounted by his successor. Thrusting. Thrusting. He squeezed the image away.

Or worse, his kids would grow up with some other guy for a dad. A better dad. A guy who wasn't a sex freak.

Terry pulled the car into the Burger King lot. A cold trickle seeped into Danny's bowels. If I died, Judy would go through all my stuff! What about my collection of favorite underwear catalogs? Judy would find them! She would discover my dirty secret. Her last thoughts of me would be filled with disgust. Well, at least it wasn't child porn or gay stroke mags. Just a sad little stack of well-thumbed catalogs. Maybe she wouldn't even understand. How could she? How could any woman know the anguish of being a man, always moving to the whip crack of testosterone? She couldn't know. I'll die with my secret. Thank God.

Only the pain in Danny's wrists, now numbing his hands, kept him from lapsing into an exhausted stupor. He was drawing deeper and deeper into himself, away from the FM radio music and cigarette smoke stinking up his beautiful car. Away from the smell of bacon and hamburger grease and french fries and onions.

"You hungry?" The girl on one side of him, the skinny straw-berry blonde, was talking. The one with the good heart.

Suddenly he was famished. He smiled back and nodded. Adelle began to feed him french fries, one by one, picking out each greasy stick with care. He felt like a goat in a petting zoo. As he chewed, Danny came to life and examined Adelle more closely. She was as fresh and flawless as only an eighteen-year-old girl can be. Her milk-pale skin was innocent of any blemish, any stress. The movement of her delicate wrists was fragile and in-complete, not pragmatic as Judy's had become running two chil-dren through their paces. Did this girl know he was watching her? She must.

Shel batted the dashboard in a jittery rhythm. "Let's go back to the fire. Let's go see what's happening!"

Beckett, his head tilted back, had his eyes closed. "What about this guy?"

Terry sucked air through the ice on the bottom of his cup. "Fuck him."

Beckett didn't move, asking his question to the ceiling. "Should we let him go?"

Terry spat an ice chip at Danny. "Nah, let's just leave him in the backseat like that and sooner or later someone will find him."

Danny thought, This is how crazy people feel, the way I feel right now.

"Terry, drive the car back to the mall and we'll just leave it there." Beckett's eyes were open. He was in command.

"What about our fingerprints?"

"No one cares about our fingerprints. And he's not going to tell anybody about us. Are you?"

"Please, just undo the seat belt." Danny was surprised by the kittenish mewl of his own voice.

Shel screamed: "I want to go look at the fire!"

"I'll stay with him."

The angelic girl who had been feeding Danny french fries was coming to his aid again! Danny dared to hope. Her misanthropic friends would wander off, bored. She would stay behind and undo the seat belt and help him escape.

The Saab wended back to the familiar parking lot. Police had been attempting roadblocks in and out of the growing circus of mayhem. But there was too much going on, the parking lot had too many entrances and exits. Too many vehicles were coming and going, including press and cops' families and owners of stores and the mall itself. The police were tired of asking questions, overcome with the fatigue fear brought. Roving bands of the curious slid back and forth across the black expanse.

Terry and the Pirates, as Danny had come to think of these kids, slipped out of the car into the night, leaving Danny alone with the girl, Adelle, the only warmhearted one of the bunch. She smiled at him. He didn't want to think about what he looked like. It didn't make any difference. The ordeal would be over soon.

43

Mal woke out of his Nosferatu sleep, covered in a cool sweat, his mind filled with nothing. Like a man in free fall writhing and grasping for handholds in the air, Mal's mind tried to establish one thing he could recognize. But all he saw was black on black. Not only did he not know where he was or what time it was, he couldn't even remember his name. He was lost. Mal could sense the pressure of the tree against the back of his head and the ground under his butt. When he tried to move his hand, he felt the weight of the pistol twisted into his stiff fingers and then suddenly, like a vast flock of birds, reality rose up, squawking and flapping.

When Mal did finally inhale, he tasted the smoke on his dry tongue, and with that taste, memory and the power of his actions flooded his veins: he was renewed, reborn. But now he was not the Mal of a few hours ago who had made a decision to do certain things. He was the Mal who had actually *done* those things. Powerful Mal, the new King of Death, Mal. Mal felt the threatening dark around him diminish and his own existence grow, a giant in a world of pygmies.

Slowly, Mal turned his head and looked behind and above where he sat, up the incline to the highway. Yes, the red and blue flashing lights were there, so patient and predictable. They were there waiting for him. The colors twinkled in his eyes.

Mal moved a leg muscle and then a red neon light in his head pulsed *caution*. Very slowly, he let his hand creep into his jacket pocket and withdrew a shotgun shell. Gently he tossed it twenty feet away and listened. Nothing. Ten full minutes passed and Mal felt nothing; not even a ripple in the air betrayed any other sentient being in this neck of the little woods.

Mal slowly rose up and, walking heel to toe just as he had learned in Scouts, made his way up the incline toward the beating lights. He stopped. Listened. Nothing. A fan belt squealed out in the parking lot. Mal kept moving. Time for the next part.

44

Adelle undid the seat belt. "Turn around," she gently instructed Danny. She examined the handcuffs one more time. It was amazing what a little plated steel could do to a human being. It was the sort of thing that happened to wild animals when they got tangled up in plastic six-pack rings or some old fishing net. Steel and plastic mesh were not natural.

Danny could feel her gentle hands touch his sore wrists, wedging one of her thin fingers under the metal rings, measuring the gap.

Feeling her gentle probing, Danny asked: "Do you have a hairpin?"

Adelle laughed sweetly. "Girls don't have hairpins these days!" He felt her touching his upper arms, then her warm breath on his neck. What is she doing? A *click*. The sound was so irrational, Danny thought he was imagining it. Then another *click*. The pain raced up Danny's arms like mad electricity as Adelle ratcheted each ring one more notch.

"What are you doing! Why did you do that?"

Concern clouded Adelle's features. "Oh, is that too tight?"

"Yeah, yeah it is! Wow. Wow. Make it go back."

A small vertical appeared between Adelle's perfect eyebrows. "I can't, they only go one way."

"It hurts! Shit!"

"It does?"

"Yes!!!!"

Through his watering eyes, Danny tried to turn and see Adelle's face. Was she smiling? No.

Adelle spun Danny around. With the placid efficiency of a Nazi doctor, she snapped the belt around him again. Her cool eyes were not the eyes of a savior.

"Don't hurt me."

Adelle smiled. She took a cigarette lighter out of her jeans pocket. Danny watched it in her hand.

Adelle smiled again and put the lighter away. "That's just a piece of information. So you have that information now. Okay? Big guy?"

"Yeah, okay. What are you going to do?"

"What do you want me to do?"

"Get the handcuffs off me."

"Well, I don't know how. So then, what do you want me to do?"

"Go away, leave me alone."

Adelle smiled again, reached into her pocket for the cigarette lighter. "Don't you like me?"

The lids of Danny's eyes drooped. "Yes."

"Do you want to make it with me?"

"I . . . what do you want me to say?"

"Tell me the truth."

Danny considered the lighter. The handcuffs were like ferrets chewing his wrists. He felt nauseous. He didn't know the answer, crazy wheels turned in his head.

"Really, tell me the truth."

"You're a very beautiful girl."

"Yes?"

"In other circumstances, like for instance if I had no handcuffs on, wasn't married and was fifteen years younger, I would want to, you know, 'be' with you."

A voice screamed inside Danny: You're good at lying, so lie! She's just a kid, make her believe you. Do whatever you have to do. Head-butt her. Bite her face.

Adelle cocked her head. "You would?"

"Yes. I'd love that."

"You can 'be' with me now."

Danny's brain fried in its juices. His voice shrunk. "I can?"

"Sure. You'd like that, wouldn't you?"

"Are you going to burn me with that lighter?"

"That's an interesting idea. Do you want me to burn you with the lighter?"

"No, of course not."

"You sure?"

"Yes, I'm sure."

Adelle reached under the seat belt and tugged at Danny's waist. He could only watch as she undid his Coach leather belt and unbuttoned the button of his Boss pants. She put her hands under his shirt and felt his belly, closing her eyes as she touched him. She smiled again.

"You're like my total slave now. Isn't that incredible? I bet you've been with hookers."

"I've never been with a hooker in my life."

"Bullshit, you're a businessman, you're with hookers all the time. I've seen you guys in movies. I know what you do."

"I've never been with a hooker or a prostitute or a massage therapist or anybody like that in my whole life. I swear. Do you believe me? Please believe me. I never hurt you."

Adelle pinched a wisp of hair below Danny's navel and pulled. "Of course you hurt me."

"Oww. Why'd you do that?"

"Because I don't like it when you lie. Do you want to kiss me?" Adelle giggled.

"No."

Adelle slapped his cheek hard.

"Do you want to kiss me?"

"Yeah."

Adelle straddled Danny, bringing the weight of his arms down harder on his wrists. He clenched his teeth. His eyes watered. Adelle pushed her soft lips onto his. She licked his teeth. She laughed a hearty laugh. "This is so cool!"

"You're breaking my arms."

"Cool."

She pressed down on him. Danny wondered if his teeth could find her neck. He wondered if his teeth could cut into her jugular. Everything went black.

45

Michel heard the tap of the shell hitting the brown leaves. The tricky fox is trying to fool me, he thought. Michel could wait too. And he did. But when the man finally did move, the mobilization was quick and smooth and in a direction Michel had not expected, up the incline toward the highway and toward the waiting police. Perhaps he was going to give himself up. Perhaps it would be over in a few minutes.

Michel, letting his prey ascend until he could no longer hear him, followed as slowly as he could. No need to hear, he could smell him. The security guard flanked the moving man, slipping along to one side of him. Michel didn't want to walk into a trap or, worse, bump into him.

Ten minutes later, Michel could see the top of the slope above him through the trees. He knew that when he got to the top, the trees would peter out, then there would be about twenty feet of grass, then the gray ribbon of guardrail, then sand, then the breakdown lane, then the paved roadway.

Michel wondered what the skinny man was doing now.

Then he heard the gunfire, heard the pops of lead hitting steel, the thuds of safety glass fracturing. Then shouts. Michel ran to the top of the slope and dropped to his belly. Like a G.I. Joe toy, he wriggled forward, holding the shotgun ahead of him. The noise stopped abruptly.

Michel peered up over the scrubby grasses that grew between the manicured highway lawn and the rubbishy growth of the sumac saplings. The skinny man was standing out in the middle of the highway. No police were to be seen. Between the man and Michel lay the shattered remains of yet another state trooper cruiser.

The world seemed to be holding its breath. If there were bodies, Michel couldn't see them. As far as Michel could see, the skinny man was completely exposed. But then why was no one shooting at him?

Michel craned his head upward, to see under the cruiser, to see the man's feet. If he could get a clear shot, the man wouldn't stand a chance. Then Michel understood why the skinny man was invulnerable. He was holding a shotgun and at his feet lay a wounded trooper, the muzzle hanging directly over his head.

Even if the skinny man caught a load cleanly in the heart, the death spasm would end the trooper's life as well. Michel looked up for the first time and saw the lights of the helicopters hanging, like ornaments suspended from the black sky.

Michel crept forward. If someone saw him now, they'd know what he was up to. In fact, there had to be men all around him, creeping forward as well. But Michel was the closest and Michel was in the position the skinny man would never suspect, directly behind him. Michel made a decision. He would get close enough and he would run at the man. The man would either have to raise his gun and shoot Michel or Michel would knock the man down. Either way, the man would die. Michel felt all his muscles clench and then, like the sun rising, something entered him and Michel moved.

46

Jeff examined the cell phone, a black gnome with a blinking green eye, beckoning him to another world. This was what he wanted, adventure, the unknown. Tonight he would pursue this woman wherever she led him. And it would be only the first step in a life that would span continents and decades as he pursued every avenue of exploit.

Jeff thought, I'm in the young man phase now. Young men have sex with anonymous women, commit petty crimes and gamble and drink too much. Taking acid is like drinking too much. After tonight I will strike out to some faraway city where I will starve for a while, then meet a mentor, a traveler like myself. I'll master some incredibly difficult skill like ice climbing or Japanese sword fighting, but never use it. Then the greater adventures will begin. All I need to have is—

The phone twittered in his hand. Jeff fumbled with the buttons. "Hello?"

A husky-voiced woman demanded, "Who's this?"

Was this Donna? Better be careful. "Uh. Alonzo."

"So, Alonzo. What are you doing?"

Jeff was pretty sure it was her. "Nothing."

"You want to do something?"

"I *guess* so."

"You guess so?"

"Yeah, I do. Uh, want to do something. Where did you go?"

"Three seventeen."

"What?"

Click.

Three seventeen. Jeff dropped the cell phone into his knapsack and popped the door. A red light on the dash began winking. Jeff wondered if Donna had taken her keys, if he'd be locking her out of her own car. She might get in trouble. Feigning recklessness, he shut the thought out of his mind.

Jeff retraced his steps along the front of the motel, past the diamond-shaped windows of the brown lounge door, entering instead the much airier, red-and-blue-accented, antiseptic-smelling foyer of the motel proper. He steeled himself for sharp-eyed inspection from a doorman or bell captain or concierge, but the place was void of service personnel.

An empty luggage cart stood alone, its brass rails scratched, the red-carpeted base scuffed and torn. Behind the reception desk a fuzzy-haired girl with bad skin murmured into the phone. Otherwise, the gleaming room was vacant. Jeff walked past a black felt signboard propped on an easel. It had movable white letters spelling out WELCOME and GREETINGS. Jeff imagined the local Lions Club and Overeaters Anonymous members sipping their coffee in the neighboring "conference rooms."

Jeff stepped into the matrix of corridors and side corridors. But instead of finding himself at a bank of elevators, he emerged at a small breakfast restaurant, now shuttered. A placard on another easel invited him to TRY THE INTERNATIONAL BUFFET! Jeff turned and retraced his steps.

The girl on the phone watched him, zombielike; only her eyes moved. Jeff could see she was writing something on a pad in front of her. Finding the turn he had missed, he hung a right, which sent him back toward the bar/restaurant. It stood waiting for him at the end of the hallway, full of familiar neon-lit darkness, beer and the aroma of grilled meat. Just before the doors to the bar, Jeff found the elevators. They were guarded by a short brushed-aluminum cylinder topped with a dish full of white sand. The sand had been embossed with the hotel logo.

Jeff tapped the elevator button. The sliding doors chimed and opened immediately, as if they had been waiting all night just for him. He stepped in. The doors came together and Jeff was surrounded by infinitely reflecting mirrors. He saw himself for the first time in hours. This is what I look like to everyone else. This is me. Wow. I look sad. My eyes are red. I'm all baggy. I'm like someone who melted.

Jeff's eyes fixed on his mirror eyes. This is me. This is my inside on the outside. This is a place I cannot escape—myself. I cannot escape myself and I cannot escape this elevator. I am locked into this moment, this self, this place forever. How did I get here? Why here and not someplace else?

Then the world narrowed down to nothing more than two sets of pupils within pupils within pupils and Jeff felt weightless. He was plummeting into his own eyes.

A familiar chime sounded and with a jerk the doors reopened. Everything snapped back as a white-haired man and a silver-haired woman, both pungent with gin, entered the elevator. The woman had a gob of guacamole running down the front of her raspberry chiffon gown. Jeff shuffled a bit to make room, at the same time noticing the first-floor foyer outside, from which he had not risen. How long had he been standing here checking himself out in the mirrors?

The white-haired man pushed a button. Then he snuck a look at Jeff and for a moment Jeff thought the man might actually be the White Rabbit in disguise, but then the man asked him simply: "Floor?"

Jeff noted tiny red squiggles on the tip of the man's nose, as if someone had taken a red ballpoint pen and doodled there. Jeff had taken the guy for some kind of executive, a guy with a corner office and a secretary. Now he realized he was just a lush on Social Security. His heart flooded with pity for the man and his old wife.

Jeff knew the answer to the man's question and gave it: "Three." The helpful ginhead pushed three and the elevator rose to the third floor. The woman gave a shy smile in Jeff's direction as if to say, "We have no money, please don't hurt us." Then the door opened and Jeff got out.

The doors closed behind him. Jeff drank in the quiet. No muzak, no sirens, no car horns, nothing. Only the stillness of musty wall-to-wall rugs in a claustrophobic, badly lit hallway. Every ten feet or so an identical lighting fixture illuminated another repeating pattern of carpet, another section of doorways, a perfect example of perspective. Someone laughed behind a door. Someone on TV.

Jeff swam along this surreal channel, thinking what a great movie set it would make, when he began to notice the numbers on the doors. More door-number reading and Jeff figured out he was headed in the wrong direction. He stopped. At his feet lay a tray piled with the ragged remains of a red and black T-bone steak, an unopened miniature bottle of A.1. sauce, salt and pepper shakers, a glass of water, a beer bottle lying on its side and a tiny vase holding one small tortured carnation. Jeff turned and plodded back to the elevators. As he did he heard the crack of a door opening, and when he reached the spill of light on the rug, he saw that the number on the door was indeed 317.

Girding himself, Jeff entered and found a miniature room engorged with a king-size bed almost touching a facing armoire. Glossy paper prop-up endorsements stood sentinel on every horizontal surface, tiny billboards of information on long-distance calling, speedy checkout, movies on pay TV and urgings to try the "international buffet." An aroma of rug shampoo hung in the air.

A hiss of running water seeped from the bathroom. Jeff closed the door of the room behind him, irrevocably sealing the sanctum where he and Donna would be transmuted. Something was about to happen to him. He didn't know what it was, but in an hour or so it would be an important memory. He was sure of that.

Jeff aimed his voice at the water music. "Hello?"

Donna's voice was brassy: "Where have you been? Get a drink."

"Okay." Like a nervous sitcom character, Jeff cleared his throat. He saw a TV set in the brown wood cabinet. He checked out the shiny, heavy coverlet tucked tightly over the bed. He inventoried one armchair, one standing lamp, two end tables, two sconce lamps and an alarm clock radio with red numerals visible. Lots of mirrors.

"Where is the drink?"

Donna emerged wearing a fluffy white robe, her calves and arms blushing from the heat of the shower. She looked like the kind of woman Jeff read about in his mother's magazines who confessed to having multiple orgasms and multiple sex partners and who enjoyed multiple "positions." The kind of woman who confessed that she was insatiable.

"Under the TV." Donna brushed past Jeff and snapped open

the cabinet, revealing a second gray door sealed with a security loop of plastic. Donna had broken the loop as she dialed her cell phone to call Jeff, so the fridge door swung open easily.

Donna and Jeff, if a bit shocked by the sensation of re-recognition, were happy to be in the water again. Donna played the friendly barmaid. "Beer? Wine? Vodka? Better stick to beer, eh?"

"Sure." Jeff felt safer with small, easy-to-pronounce words.

Donna bent and rummaged. Without looking up, she thrust a hard-on–size cardboard tube up at Jeff's face. "You want a Toblerone, too? Give you energy?"

"Sure."

Jeff grabbed the candy bar like a lifeline. Not sure what to do next, he plopped down in the little armchair and tore off the triangular cardboard and foil. He bit into the waxy chocolate as Donna brought him his beer. For a moment, he wasn't sure if he had enough hands.

To Donna, Jeff appeared scruffier, but then she transposed his skinniness to lankiness, his rawness into virility and his youth into beauty. Her mind's eye flipped through an album of movie stars, finally fixing on Brad Pitt in *Thelma and Louise*. That worked.

Jeff realized she was still standing over him. He should say something. "You look good."

"So do you."

"Where's the remote control for the TV?"

"You bored with me already? You wanna watch some porno?"

"Porno?"

"All the rooms have piped-in porno, for the lonely salesmen on the road."

"Porno is fucked up. I don't like it."

Donna moved closer, interrupting Jeff before he could explain. "What *do* you like?"

Donna touched the back of his neck. Jeff could smell her clean skin beaming through the terry cloth. The mounds of her breasts stood just above his eyeline so when he looked up at her face he had to look past them. The chocolate slipped out of his hand, and for a moment Jeff wondered if it would be edible after lying on the carpet. All kinds of things had been spilled or secreted in this room. Now he was making his contribution.

Jeff put one arm around Donna's thighs and buttocks. He pulled her toward him and to his shock, as he flattened his cheek into the robe, he could detect a faint aroma of sex through the pristine cotton. His tongue worked a piece of chocolaty nut stuck between molars.

Donna drew Jeff up out of the chair and they kissed again, mouths open. There was no invisible parking lot chaperone now, now they could kiss for real. Jeff felt her strength. Even her tongue was strong. She tasted and felt like a grown-up, her body strong and enveloping. Her robe opened and Jeff pressed his grungy clothes into her warm skin.

Donna attended to her mission with vigor. She pulled at his rags, finding the buttons and zippers, seeking the naked boy under the armor of cool. Her appetite had let loose something bigger than her normal self. She was no more in control than when she rode the Crazy Mouse at the fairgrounds.

Jeff turned and through the sheer curtains covering the large window he could see the flickering colors of the mall across the way. For a moment he wanted to be over there, where things were sad but not so complicated. Donna tumbled him backward onto the bed.

The kissing became a kind of fucking. Like twin Houdinis, Donna and Jeff extricated themselves from their clothing while bound at the mouth, until they were simply two half-naked people huffing and grappling. Jeff's mind raced. He imagined his dick being rolled up against a launch gantry, tall and proud, independent and as far away as Cape Canaveral.

He had to make decisions. Should he keep kissing her for a while, then try to touch her breasts? What about the fact that his pants were now binding his ankles together? What if she had some kind of sexually transmitted disease? What if he got her pregnant? Should he try to touch her between the legs? What would she think if he did that? What if he farted?

As Jeff's mind and body found the going complex and rigorous, Donna proceeded along the friendly familiar path, one she had been down hundreds of times with Roy. She didn't ponder it, it was just the way it was, like changing the oil in your car. First you did this, then you did that. Unscrew this nut, pull that lever.

Guys she was with shouldn't have to do anything in particular but lay back and function. It was her job to get everything stiffened and aligned properly and it was the guy's job, if she was lucky, to jostle forward and back. Donna liked it this way.

So she gently pushed Jeff onto his back, pulled his pants off his ankles, rubbed his chest, brought her cheek to his belly and, looking coyly up into his eyes, put his cock between her lips. She suckled on him for a while while making noises of pleasure, came up for air once, sucked him some more and then finally rose up, threw one heavy leg over his inert body, straddled him, took his springy, hard penis in her hand and stuck it into herself.

The slightest friction only made the pleasure blossom harder for Jeff. Then something inside Donna released and everything loosened and pulsed with slick goodness. Jeff's anxiety dispersed. Waves of astoundingly good sensations rippled through him and he floated along in the warm current like a blissed-out, slightly stunned tuna.

Before this, Jeff had only known cramped, hurried, confused sex. So after a few minutes of soothing copulation, Jeff contemplated his situation and was pleased. As Donna bobbed over him, he let his eyes roam the room, taking in the framed Americana prints on the wall, the smoke detector on the ceiling and the little freestanding bit of shiny cardboard on the nightstand surveying his satisfaction with his stay. He giggled inside himself.

After a bob or two, being nineteen, Jeff should have shot his load. But tonight, his dick seemed miles away, touristing around some fascinating foreign land. Donna, the unaware actor in her own scenario, bounced up and down on his sex gristle, threw her head back and growled, "Oh Jesus, oh Jesus, oh Jesus. Yeah. Fuck me! Fuck me!" He didn't have to move at all.

The rhythm, instead of bringing Jeff to an orgasm, lulled him into a Zen-like state of mind. Donna began scratching him and swearing and whipping her head around. Although Jeff had never seen his girlfriend doing anything like this, he figured this meant she was having an orgasm. As Donna became more histrionic, Jeff became more curious and less aroused. Finally, in a shuddering fit of passion, Donna hollered her way through three orgasms and collapsed onto him, slippery with sweat. Her insides clenched him in a little happy rhythm. Jeff went completely soft and plopped out.

Almost panting, Donna lay on top of Jeff, her heavy breasts warming his chest. She was kissing his neck very gently now, still talking, saying things like, "Oh, yeah . . . yeah that was great." Jeff held her, but instead of feeling like the debauched young man, he assumed the role of the jaded old rake who had taken advantage of the naïve ingenue. The heat of her breasts and belly aroused him again. Donna rolled onto her back, her eyes glazed. She murmured: "That was good. Was it good for you? You didn't make much noise."

"That's 'cause I didn't come."

"Yes, you did."

"No. I didn't."

"Oh, wow. Well, we'll have to take care of that."

Donna gripped Jeff in a way he had never been held before, twisted his dick like an old-fashioned radio dial and in no more than sixty seconds had him squirting his load. In the chilly motel air, the semen puddled on the oyster-colored sheets, leaving Jeff as melancholy as a cow.

"There, that better?"

"What happened?"

"Didn't you like it?"

Jeff lay drained in complete nonsatisfaction. He could feel the gooseflesh rising on his arms. His mouth was dry and sour and he could smell his sweaty, vodka-soaked companion lying next to him.

Jeff contemplated Donna's face. Her eyes were closed but he knew she wasn't asleep. He felt a twinge of paranoia or at least what he thought paranoia would feel like. They were only strangers.

He wondered where Adelle was.

47

Danny was suspended between heaven and hell. He had been with Judy. It wasn't a dream because there was none of the gauzy pleasure of a dream. He and Judy were in a concentration camp, being tortured. The storm troopers were forcing them to have sex with each other. As he humped her bony body, he could feel the dirt under his knees and the bayonets scratching his back. Guttural chuckles behind him followed his every downstroke. He was fucking Judy and all he could think was, We finally get to have sex and it has to be like this. Danny rose up through the murky depths of his hallucination, falling backward into the crisp and nasty present. He tried to fight it off, but reality would not be denied.

He was back in the car with Adelle. Although he had now lost all sensation in his arms, his shoulders were riddled with pain. At the same time he knew he was erect and his balls were on fire. All the juice that had stored up while he was watching Donna now boiled in his groin, demanding to be let out. As he opened his eyes, the first thing he saw was Adelle's delicate hand squeezing his balls and stroking his dick. He was in agony.

She looked up at him, as if he were her science project. Danny was the class frog and Adelle was leading the experiment. "Run the wires from the battery, see the legs twitch!" She pulled and pulled, shoving him incrementally toward orgasm.

Adelle searched Danny's tormented eyes. He was completely under her control. She stopped. Danny, who had been trying to hold back, maintain his last molecule of dignity, didn't understand. Adelle watched him. One small syllable escaped from Danny's lips.

"No."

"What? You want me to keep going?"

"Please, let me go."

"We're here. This is it. So what do you want?"

"I feel stupid."

"You are stupid. You're a stupid man. You're an ugly, stupid man."

"I'm not."

"Shut up!" Adelle slapped Danny again. His life force left him and he let his head hang. But his dick stayed hard.

"What do you want. Tell me!" Adelle's smile was a witch's grimace.

"Stop torturing me."

"You want me to make you come?"

"Yes."

Adelle grabbed his dick and yanked it. "Like this?"

"No."

"Say: 'I'm a pervert.'"

"No."

"Say it."

Danny could not believe he was in reality. So it made no difference what he said. "I'm a pervert."

"Say it over and over."

She stroked his penis as he repeated the mantra and finally, without bliss, Danny shot his wad as Adelle held his penis and tried to aim it at his face.

"Yech!!! You're gross!" Adelle wiped her hand on Danny's Egyptian cotton shirt. She opened the door of the car.

"Where are you going?"

Adelle turned and smiled: " 'Bye, it was nice meeting you."

"Put my pants back on! Wipe me off!"

Adelle slammed the door behind her. Danny lay slumped in the dark, eyes closed, his wilting dick already drying. He wondered if there was a way to kill himself. Sooner or later, someone would find this car and open the door and he would be in the backseat, trussed in a seat belt and handcuffed, his arms paralyzed forever, his pants open, his body exposed. Danny opened his eyes and the first thing he saw was his slack penis. He spoke to it, a good friend who had betrayed him.

"I hate you."

48

Jeff spoke to Donna's shuttered lids: "Do you want to do it again?"

Thick, dreamy: "Sure." Donna's eyes stayed closed.

Jeff watched the expansion and contraction of her perfectly formed rib cage, her centerfold breasts, her flat belly.

Donna opened her eyes.

"Gimme your number."

"My number?"

"So we can get together again."

"I meant, right now. Did you want to do it again right now?"

"Right now? When I'm feeling all cozy and finalized? I dunno. It's been a long day and I have to get home to my hubby and rug-rat. Maybe next time."

Donna found her drink on the nightstand and took a swallow. She sat up. "I think I saw aspirin in the mini-bar. You still have that phone?"

A puff of air conditioner–chilled air grazed Jeff's body, drying his skin. He rummaged the phone out of his knapsack and handed it to Donna. He retrieved his briefs and pulled them on.

Donna rolled off the bed and hit the speed dial as she flat-footed her way over to the mini-fridge. She didn't mind being naked in front of Jeff. Her tits and ass weren't, like they were for some women, who she *was*.

The antiseptic flavor of the room returned.

Jeff clicked on the TV. As Donna crunched Advils, he rolled through channels, finding coverage of the fire and shootings at the mall. A lost orphan chain of lysergic acid molecules teased his cortex as he compared the live image from the helicopters above with the actual business only a few hundred yards away. Jeff sensed Donna behind him, talking to someone on the phone, probably her husband.

"I was up at the mall shopping and a fire broke out and the police rounded everybody up and questioned them and . . . well, I'm in my car right now, but they're not letting any cars leave just yet. I know, baby, I know. What did you give him? Well, that's good, fried chicken's nutritious. Oh, don't let Randy in the house. I know, I know, but he went down in the swamps again and he stinks. Well, then just lock him down in the garage. No. Don't worry about it, I'll deal with it tomorrow. Okay. Okay. I love you too."

Jeff stroked Donna's foot as he watched the TV. At first, the stroking was gentle and affectionate, but the longer she blabbed with her husband, the more rhythmic and expressionless his touch became. By the time she hung up, he could have been fondling a piece of driftwood. On the TV screen, jittery images of fire and smoke and firefighters and milling onlookers montaged with ads for cereal and cheeseburgers. Donna tugged her foot to herself and Jeff hunched forward focusing on the TV.

"Have they said how many got killed?" Donna could have been asking about the weather report.

Jeff didn't turn to address her, only hunkered more tightly toward the screen. "It's a rampage. So far eight people are dead."

"No. Right over there? That's terrible."

"Yeah."

Donna stood up and sorted her clothes, finding her nefarious panties. She pulled them on and smiled at Jeff.

"You're really good, you know that?" She pushed him back onto the bed and kissed him quick and hard before bouncing up and away.

Jeff closed his eyes and listened to the rustle of Donna dressing. A mantle of incomprehension draped over his mind. Colors swam behind his eyelids. He didn't like this room, he didn't like what was on the TV and he didn't like Donna. The lusciousness of her body was no more than a glossy two-dimensional pullout. Only the staples were missing. He surprised himself when he imagined hitting her.

Donna fussed in front of a mirror. "Honey, I gotta get going. Roy's worried about me."

Jeff didn't open his eyes. Donna mistook his sulking for drunkenness. "But listen, see, this room is on my credit card? So you have to leave now too. Okay, baby?"

"Why? You already paid for it."

"Yes, but, you know, what if you trashed the place? Then I'd have to pay for the damage."

"Why would I do that?"

Donna stood before Jeff's flaccid, sprawling self. "Could you look me in the eyes for a sec, honey?"

Jeff opened his eyes and there was Donna, all put back together, looking exactly as she had when she spoke to him in the bar. A blip of dirty sex thoughts appeared and disappeared. Nothing was going to happen now. He had served his function and she was on her way down to the parking lot. All valence between them was grounded.

"What if you decided to drink everything in the mini-bar?" Donna knew how to run an interrogation. She'd had plenty of practice with Roy Jr.

"I've had enough to drink."

Donna picked the broken chocolate bar off the floor and tossed it into the wastebasket under the desk. "But I'm saying, why do you want to stay in here? To watch TV?"

"I dunno, I'm kind of comfortable."

"Maybe you're gonna go down to the bar and pick up another innocent girl, huh?"

Jeff looked up at Donna blankly. "What?"

Where was this kid's sense of humor? There was something she didn't get about him and that gave him the upper hand.

"So, like I said, I gotta run. What's your phone number?"

"It's okay. You don't have to call me."

"But I had such a great time!"

"I bet we run into each other again. Or maybe not."

"Yeah."

Donna walked over to Jeff and stroked his hair. She bent over and kissed him. "You're a bad dude. I'm not gonna be able to walk tomorrow." Donna saw a flash cross Jeff's face just like the flash before Roy threw her hair dryer that time. "Okay, gotta go. Love ya."

Jeff heard the door open and close. He was alone with the TV and the window and the mini-bar. He got up from the bed, picked up the robe where Donna had dropped it and stuck his arms in the sleeves. A vestige of Donna's scent clung to the fabric.

Enrobed and still high, Jeff sat like this for ten minutes. Then he wandered into the bright bathroom with the endlessly whirring exhaust fan and the collection of small bottles: lotion, shampoo, conditioner. The free shower cap. The unwrapped bar of soap from Donna's pre- and postcoital scrub. Outside in the hallway, he heard a room service cart rumble by, glasses tinkling. Then nothing.

Back in the room proper, the artwork on the wall troubled Jeff. He touched one of the framed prints and found it had been screwed to the wall, as if someone might want to take it as a memento of their stay in this upholstered cage. He lay his fingers along the top edge of the painting, gave it a hard yank and managed to pry it off the wall. He left it hanging out at an angle, crippled and wrong.

Jeff unplugged a lamp from the end table and carried it into the bathroom. He tossed it into the bathtub. The lamp slid down the hard molded plastic of the tub's contours. It stopped over the drain hole, the lampshade buckling slightly. Jeff wandered back into the bedroom.

Out of the mini-bar, Jeff removed two pygmy fifths of Cutty Sark and a bottle of Heineken, settled back in front of the TV and started to "flip around."

A ball game was in progress. Bright colors and men glowering at one another. Jeff could not decipher it. He focused as hard as he could on a skinny black guy holding a bat. Jeff decided the guy should have a home run. Jeff thought, Home run. Then, with a corkscrew wallop, the skinny black guy hit one out. As the white speck sailed off toward the scrambling bleacher weirdos, Jeff nodded to himself. He took a sip from his drink in self-congratulation.

Flip, flip. A voice in an English accent spoke over a black-and-white film. Soldiers in tattered uniforms walked past other men in civilian dress. The civilians held rifles. The soldiers were carrying things, dragging things. They were throwing floppy things into a huge pit. The things were fish-belly-white bodies of humans. Jeff pressed the soft rubber button, extinguishing the horror.

Men sitting at desks were insulting each other. Laugh track. Naked animosity. More laughter. Flip. Flip.

The fire came into helicopter view. Police and onlookers swarmed like ants. The footage cut again and the helicopter revealed a fifteen-mile backup on the highway, long parallel lines of red and white. Jeff heard the words *fifteen-mile backup.* It felt so far away Jeff felt nostalgic.

Jeff pushed the MENU button on the remote control, selected the "mature movies" ($10.95, "Movie title will not appear on your bill!"), fluffed the pillows and settled back to watch two naked women tussle and lick each other.

Jeff remembered his drinks and poured the baby bottles of booze into the Heineken, spilling some over himself and onto the bed. He lay back and like an infant sucked down about half the bottle. The smudgy colors of his LSD trip, which had died down during sex with Donna, flared and danced. As Jeff watched the hard bodies writhe, he thought, I'm alone now in a way I've never been. He smiled to himself.

Jeff dropped the robe, pulled the coverlet off the bed and snuggled down between the clean white hotel sheets, making a womb. He sucked on his beer-and-whiskey teat and cuddled the hard foam pillows. Eyelids at half mast, he let the wash of chemicals in his bloodstream take him as onscreen one woman strapped on a massive multicolored dildo. She started ramming it into the ass of the other, but because it was hotel porn, the actual penetration had been edited out. The women struggled with their orgasms as if being exorcised, groaning and screaming, their faces taut.

A new scene began around a ranch house surrounded by lush banana leaves and palms. Must be California, thought Jeff. A man in a hard hat was knocking on a door and a woman wearing a pink terry towel tube thing invited him in. She led him to a patioed backyard and medium-size swimming pool. They made poorly acted small talk for a few minutes. Soon the man, still wearing his hard hat, and the woman, now naked, were in the swimming pool pouring water over each other and fucking.

Jeff caught a glimpse of the man's penis and it seemed too large to be real. The woman's breasts were too round and she had no pubic hair. They were both tanned, the man had a rippling abdomen and big pecs. Who were these people? The way they had sex wasn't like any sex he knew and the groaning and noise was . . . well, Donna had sounded a bit like that.

"Jeff?"

Jeff heard his name being spoken.

"Jeff, it's us."

Jeff was distracted by some beer spilled on the sheets and had been observing the liquid spread over and absorb into the almost white fabric. He looked up to see faces crowded into the frame of the TV screen, all watching him.

A very tan, naked girl with a large mouth was speaking.

"Jeff, are you okay?"

"No. I'm not okay. I'm fucked up."

"We're your friends. We'll help you."

The naked men and women were climbing out and through the screen of the TV and into bed with Jeff. They were holding him, consoling him. Out the window Jeff could see that the flames of the mall had grown and now filled the entire sky, licking the windows of the motel. He could smell coconut oil. Long hair brushed against his face. Someone was stroking his back.

The porn stars embraced his bony limbs. They poured lotion on his tight skin and rubbed. They kissed his legs, his arms, his eyes. Warm skin caressed and pressed against him. Someone was whispering sweetly in his ear. He couldn't understand the words, but he knew what they meant.

The tension untangled and drifted away. Jeff felt good. He understood: love was all the world needed and it didn't make any difference if malls burned or cops got killed (after you wished them dead) or housewives took advantage of you. Everything was good, everything was good when you loved. God is love. God is everywhere.

The supple hands and legs and lips pulled him upward. He floated, the sheets stirring in the breeze. The window cracked and mall fire leaked into the room and Jeff watched the walls blacken and catch fire. The bed was getting scorched. Jeff thought, Good thing I'm not on the bed anymore.

The blaze leapt up, trying to touch Jeff's floating body. A corner of the sheet browned, then with a flutter lit on fire. The sheet puckered up in flame. The bed disappeared behind an incandescent veil.

Water was needed. Jeff somersaulted over the top of the wall, into the bathroom, and, as fast as he could reach down, turned the shower on full force. The flame and the water battled. Jeff tossed about in a maelstrom of red and blue. In the end, the water won. Water always wins, Jeff thought. Why? Why does it win? What is winning? When will I win? I don't care. I don't care. Soaked and exhausted, he saw the filled bath below him and swan-dived down into the warm liquid.

The bathtub was much larger than he remembered it. The lamp had somehow disappeared, so he was free to do a few laps. Back and forth he swam, finally becoming so tired he just turned over and let himself float. The sun was setting. Somewhere the sun was setting, he thought. The sun was always setting somewhere. But it's also rising too.

49

In the middle of the highway, in the middle of the knot of roadways and fast-food outlets, in the middle of the county, in the middle of the state, even in the middle of the continent, stood Mal, shotgun in hand, ready to pull the trigger. Like a giant steel wheel, everything was turning and Mal was the axle.

Surrounded by police cars, onlookers, video crews and helicopters overhead, Mal was going to die soon, he knew that. He was in an altered state few people other than Mongol warriors and kamikaze pilots and Manson family members had ever known. His blood was thick with the gratification of murder. There was no way to turn back, for him or his victims. No one could take that away from him, no matter how many times they killed him.

And there was always the possibility he wouldn't die. He wondered, if he dropped the weapon and lay face down on the asphalt right now, while the cameras filmed, if he wouldn't just be whisked away like Kaczynski or McVeigh, unharmed, in fact, protected by the very forces surrounding him at this moment. That would be ironic. But not as good as what was coming.

Mal kept pressure on his trigger finger. He wasn't sure what would happen if he took a sniper's bullet directly to the brain, if he would simply collapse or spin around or implode with so much pain he wouldn't be able to think of anything else. But as far as he knew, there was some possibility he would spasm and yank the trigger and blow away the trooper lying at his feet. He knew that even if that were no more than a ten percent chance, that was enough to hold at bay all the rifles which had him in their crosshairs right now.

Only a few hours ago, Mal had been watching television. Now he *was* the TV show and people all over the country had to watch *him*. Everyone wondering who he was. Maybe FBI specialists were profiling him or perhaps they had already figured him out. Run the license plate. Found out where he lived. Interviewed the neighbors.

His mother's house had probably burned down by now, but there was no way they would have found her body. Before he torched the house, he should have dragged an armchair out on the front lawn and tossed her in it and driven away. Well, you can't think of everything.

A gap opened in Mal's train of cognition. He tried to retrace, remember his last thought. Couldn't. He heard a grunt from the man at his feet and contemplated the back of the trooper's skull, where the muzzle of the shotgun rested. Yeah. Two hours ago you were writing a seventy-five-dollar ticket with your merciless, fish-eyed cop attitude, he thought. Now you got your face in the dirt, thinking about all the ways your brains can splatter. Now you're a chickenshit like the rest of us.

There wasn't much the trooper could do. Mal had cuffed his hands behind his back and tied a belt around his ankles. Guy couldn't believe how fast Mal moved. Here we are, thought Mal, here we fucking are. One minute you're on the top of the world and then *bam,* you're flat on your belly button with a gun barrel behind your ear.

The police had been trying to get Mal's attention over the loudspeakers for at least fifteen minutes but he knew what to do with that. Nothing. He knew they were out there, sneaking around, discussing him on their walkie-talkies. He knew the specialists were lying on their stomachs, their elbows locked, eyes pressed into eyepieces. Each sharpshooter wanted nothing more than to send a round somersaulting through his skull, homogenizing his brains like the Halloween pumpkins he and his buddies would hurl skyward, weightless for a second before smashing into pulp. They'd just have to wait before they got to do that.

Mal began the final stage of his plan. He moved the shotgun to his left hand and with his right he dug the large pistol out from its holster. A TV helicopter droned overhead. Mal knew from his studies of the Vietcong that hitting a helicopter wasn't easy but there were a couple of things you could do that would bring it down. You could spray a stream of bullets into its path and it would fly into the stream and get shot to pieces.

Or you could hit the stabilizing rotor in the rear. Once the rear rotor froze, the helicopter would spin faster and faster in an opposite direction to its main rotor. In about fifteen seconds, it would spin out of control and crash. Since these helicopters were hovering, the first option wasn't worth the bother. On the other hand, there was a probability, however slight, that Mal could pin the tail on the donkey. The fireball would make great footage for news shows all around the world. Icing on the cake.

Mal shifted his weight, turned his head. Perhaps twenty men surrounded him, aiming their weapons, moving in tiny increments. As he let his eyes drop down to the roof of the police car next to which he stood, one of the searchlights on the copter overhead flashed past him and illuminated the woods from which he had stepped. In that split second, Mal saw something, something recognizable. His nemesis, the Head.

This Head was familiar to Mal. This was the Head that was peeking at him in the mall corridor when he was standing over dead, fat Barry. This was the Head that appeared at the back door of Tuxedo Time. Mal was sure he had shot and killed this Head.

A disturbing particle of thought entered Mal's mind. Whatever had happened back in the woods had something to do with this Head. This Head was attached to a man and this man was following him. Why? Why would someone go through so much trouble? Did he know this guy? Was this someone he had fucked with once? The calculations were exhausting. This Head did not fit into the plan. Mal wasn't feeling happy anymore, he was getting pissed off.

Mal's mind-set, so perfectly glued together with blood and Oreos, speed and fire, suddenly became as fragile as a bubble. His fingers tightened on each trigger, shotgun and pistol. The ravenous anger ate all his other thoughts. Fuck, fuck, fuck, fuck, fuck, fuck, fuck, fuck!!!!

Then Mal abandoned his perfect plan. Instead of aiming his pistol at the helicopter rotor and making it fall out of the sky into a fiery heap, he dropped his arm and aimed it at the Head in the woods. But the searchlight had moved and he could no longer see the Head. All the reference points in his mind began to float freely: helicopter, Head, trooper on the ground, guns in hand. Mal lost all sense of how to weigh his chances one against the next. His mind unspooled, his flawless plan fell apart and Mal began firing the .38 into the darkness.

50

The rounds cut the air over his head as Michel hugged the ground. He counted the reports. Six, seven, then eight, nine . . . could there be more than nine rounds? No. None had hit Michel. He was invulnerable. The blood roared in his chest, this was the moment. Michel gripped his shotgun, rolled a few feet to his right. He was invisible now, the helicopter's rushing clatter washing away any sound he was making. Michel stood and ran toward the skinny man.

Michel was invisible to Mal, a black man running against a backdrop of black trees. But as Michel was halfway to Mal, another searchlight made a pass and in a blink Michel was a black man bleached with incandescence, outlined by black trees.

Mal dropped the empty Colt and pulled out the Smith & Wesson under his right armpit. To do this, he had to shift the shotgun and use his left hand. Michel raised his shotgun and aimed at Mal.

Mal fired the .22 at the Head. Three rounds missed. One grazed Michel's skull. One pierced his leg.

Michel hit the skinny man in the shoulder and spun him

around, pulling Mal off the crosshairs of the scope of the marks-man who had pulled a trigger when Mal's shotgun muzzle drifted away from the trooper's head. Then Michel stumbled. The head wound didn't really hurt him, but his femoral artery was sliced in two, making one leg useless. It folded under him and Michel fell face first into the scrubby grass.

Mal pulled the trigger of the shotgun, the explosive swarm of shot removing the trooper's right hand. Instantly, Mal's invulner-ability was gone. He crouched and ran toward the woods again. Like a drop of mercury he slithered into the darkness.

All Mal had now was his .22 and some rounds in his pocket. He was no more than meat and bones and fatigue, bleeding with a shoulder wound. Running straight toward where Michel lay in the weeds, he wanted to kill the Head right then and there. Kill this boogie man. If Death was looking for him, Mal was ready. But the searchlight had shifted again and Mal was blind to the black man in the blackness.

51

As Jeff walked along the highway, he enjoyed the dance of the helicopters. Strings attached to his eyes pulled everything he saw toward the center of his vision and a news helicopter and a police helicopter almost collided. Jeff could feel everything orbiting him, all was here only for his amusement.

Jeff wasn't sure what he should do now. Should he go home? In a way he was needed here. And the prospect of scarfing down a bowl of Wheaties in the close bacon fat / old fruit peel / air freshener atmosphere of his mom's kitchen would be kind of a defeat. Jeff had to stay. The mall was sucking him back in.

The building was getting locked up more and more tightly. Some kind of climax was approaching. The entrance ramps were guarded, so Jeff skirted that approach, walked past the car dealership under the overpass of the interstate and now, since the police couldn't watch every square inch of the area, had made his way into the thinly wooded perimeter of the mall abutting the highway.

Jeff figured he could trek through the woods, come out the

other side onto the mall parking lot and be able to regroup with
Adelle and the rest, if they were still here. They were probably
wondering where he went. If he found them they could all take
off for the woods, maybe get some more beer and sit around and
talk about all that had happened. He'd have a good story for
them. One that Beckett couldn't top.

He would see Adelle again. In a way, he had changed and matured since he last saw her. I'm not the boy she mocked a few
hours ago. She would see him in a new light. He would see *her* in
a new light. She wouldn't be as intimidating. She was only a girl
and she was vulnerable too.

He would find her and his new experience would show itself
on his face and Adelle would be intrigued. She'd sit beside him
and want to know why he was so quiet. He'd let her do the talking and he would ask the difficult questions. They'd walk off into
the night, find someplace dark where they could be alone. Jeff
would confess his transgressions to Adelle, tell her about Donna.
She'd be hurt, but then he'd fold her into his arms, hold her close
and kiss her wet eyes and things would be as they should be.

The woods were larger than they had seemed from a distance.
Jeff found himself unable to find a path leading to the parking lot
and instead threaded deeper and deeper into the darkness, aware
of the police cars on the interstate above him to his right. He was
headed north, he knew that much, he could smell the cloying
smoke.

Jeff tried to peer into the darkness before him. Dozens of
neon boxes swam within boxes, circles within circles. He looked
up at the sky and something passed over him, a slow-moving
plane. Is there such a thing? Must have been another helicopter.
Searchlights skimmed the edges of the woods up by the highway.

Jeff stopped and listened, inventoried the things he could hear.
Cars coming and going. Another dog barking. A police radio.

The rattle of equipment being lifted and carried. A siren, but not nearby. A shout. The thrum of helicopters hanging in the blackness overhead. The humidity and highway vapor cushioned the clamor in a fog of warm damp poison. Then Jeff heard something else.

A tapping in the twigs and leaf litter. Probably a possum or a raccoon out for the night. But each crunch was heavy and distinct, not squirrelly and wandering. This was not the sound of a small mammal. This was the sound of a large mammal, a man, walking toward him.

Jeff knew who it was. Adrenaline exploded in his chest like fireworks. Or was he hallucinating? He held his breath as the steps made their way toward him. Closer and closer they thumped and crunched. Jeff strained to see in the dark, then, realizing he was looking in the wrong direction by about fifteen degrees, shifted his gaze and there, darkness outlined by dark gray, was a man.

He was making his way toward Jeff, as if drawn to him. Twenty-five feet away, but moving slowly and with no attempt to be quiet, steps heavy and slow. Fifteen feet and now Jeff could see the man's bowed head. He seemed to be missing an arm. Ten feet and Jeff could see he had one hand up, holding his shoulder. Jeff turned, willing himself to run. Before he could, he heard a thump, an exhalation of breath, followed by silence.

Jeff froze. The man still didn't know he was here. Jeff slowly turned around and, of course, the man was gone. Or not standing anymore. Jeff looked down and could see the figure on the ground. He waited and watched it.

"Help me."

The man was speaking to Jeff. Jeff said nothing in reply.

"I know you're there, fucker. I have a .22 pointed at your belly button. Help me."

Jeff figured he could run and the man could never hit him. But there was always the possibility that he might nick his spine and leave Jeff paralyzed forever. Jeff remained frozen.

"Asshole, I'm talking to you. I know you're not a cop, 'cause you woulda shot me by now."

"I'm not a cop."

"Oh, you're a kid. Good. Come over here."

Jeff, vibrating with cardiac rhythm, stepped closer and with each step the man and his form became clearer and sharper, developing like a photograph in solution.

Mal was propped up on his good elbow. In his right hand was the revolver pointed at Jeff. His left shoulder was blackened and stains melted down over his clothing. "Some spade shot me. My shoulder is full of buckshot. Nine hundred pigs around here and I get shot by a spade. Sit down."

Jeff sat down.

"Somewhere around here is an M-16 and a bag of ammo. Now I can't find it. You're gonna find it. Okay?"

"Sure."

"What's your name?"

"Jeff."

"Figures."

"Why does it figure?"

"Shuddup. I killed a shitload of people tonight. You don't have any speed on ya, do ya?"

"No."

"Fucking asshole."

"You're the guy who lit up the mall." Jeff understood this was an opportunity he would never get again. Ask questions. Talk. Mal didn't answer.

"I saw the fire. I saw the dead people."

"You did? Really? How'd they look?"

"Their faces were squished."

"I bet."

"Why did you shoot them?"

Mal had nothing to say.

"I used to work in this mall. You could have shot me." Jeff could feel his teeth chatter as the words left his mouth. Keep talking.

Mal's voice was a low growl. "Where'd you work?"

"In the food court, at Taco Tonight." Now Jeff felt his legs shaking.

"I never ate that shit. In fact, I never ate at the food court 'cause they didn't have the fuckin' food court when I used to work here. Just the Friendly's. Used to get the tuna melt. I figured tuna was good for me, you know? Here I am, all these years of eating tuna fish and look at me. Didn't do any good at all."

"Uh-huh."

"Shit, I'm tired. You sure you don't have some white cross or something?"

"We had some acid earlier. Beckett has the rest."

"That's just what I need, acid."

Jeff tried to think of a question. "Where'd you work?"

"Tuxedo Time."

"I've never been in there."

"The world is starving to death and that fat fuck was getting rich off renting stupid-looking clothing to other fat fucks. Complete and utter worthless bullshit."

"Yeah. That's the way I look at it." Maybe Jeff could befriend this killer, lead him out of the woods?

"Who fucking cares the way you look at it?" Mal shifted his weight. "I also killed my mother tonight. But nobody knows about that. Well, now you do."

"How'd you decide to do that?" Talking was better than not talking.

"I was bored. I figured it would be fun. It was."

"Fun?" Jeff's head swam.

"Killing people is fun. You should try it sometime."

"Would you kill me?"

"Sure."

Jeff's right leg started making little jerks. "Why don't I go find your machine gun and then in exchange for that, you let me go?"

"Are you trying to fuck with my head? Don't fuck with my head, asshole."

"No. I don't really care one way or the other."

"Yeah, well, I gotta lie down for a second here, but don't move, just sit there. While I think."

Mal lay back on the dry leaves, gripping the .22. His hand trembled as he pointed the revolver at Jeff. His muscles had no more to give him. "Fucking nigger shot me. Followed me all the way from the mall and shot me. Why? Why would he do something like that?"

"Nigger?"

"Black guy. Negro. Where'd he come from?"

"I don't know. I know one kid who's black but he doesn't come to the mall. His parents have too much money."

"Yeah, well, that's the whole problem, isn't it?"

Mal closed his eyes. The .22 drooped and finally touched the ground. Jeff waited. Mal rolled over on his stomach and farted.

52

Inside the gray sweetbreads packing Mal's skull, the synthetic chemistry fueling his V-8 soul was dissipating. The center was losing its grip and letting go. Like a glacier finally reaching the ocean, shearing off in huge chunks and floating off in the choppy brine of the current, Mal was still dangerous, but no longer coherent.

Mal perched in the darkness, ate psychic popcorn and watched as the towering walls of ice fissured and crashed. He grinned as floes of broken crystal cascaded over skullcap cliffs. The burning frozen shards were prisms. Eye-piercing color shot off the sharp edges like acrobatic straight razors tumbling through space. Mal drooled with delight.

It got better. The baby bird hit the windshield again and again, fragmented and disappeared into the blackness. A hallelujah chorus of voices harmonized between the bloody pieces of ice, a choir running scales. Over the bass thunder of the falling chunks, a television babble peppered the air with Mal's name, overheating the endless bird blood which merged with the ice and flowed over the edge.

Flesh was only an obstacle to greater and greater acceleration. With acceleration, the blaring TV voices, the pounding arteries, the roaring pulse catalyzed into a final chain reaction. The massive turbines of Mal's physiology were reaching white-hot torque and melting down.

But Mal didn't know about any of that. All he knew was the movie was so good he didn't want to bother getting up to take a leak. He wasn't surprised when he felt the warm piss run down his leg.

53

Danny wasn't listening anymore. He had been trying to follow sounds for a while, but he wasn't sure what he was hearing. So instead, he had been staring at a shirt button.

Every morning when he got ready to start his day, he touched each one of these buttons on his shirt. And every morning, unconsciously, he thought the same thought. He thought about how fine these buttons were. Other people had buttons made of plastic. But his buttons were made of shell. Someone, somewhere had meticulously shaped each little white disc. Someone else had sewn each disc to his perfectly stitched shirt. For him. All that for him. They had woven the cloth, they had folded it so neatly. So neatly.

Danny couldn't take his eyes off the button, now undone, barely attached to his rumpled and cum-stained shirt. He wanted the button to take him away from all this. Take him back to the time when the button made him happy. But the button would never make him happy again.

The pain was twisted around his body like barbed wire. He

had no more thoughts. He had no more tears. All he could do was focus on the good button. And now he could see a little face in the button. It was Judy smiling at him. Sweet, sweet Judy. His wife, his love.

Maybe someday, when he was in prison or in the mental institution or wherever he ended up, Judy would come and visit him. Maybe she would smile at him. Or sing him a lullaby. That would be good. He wouldn't need much. He didn't deserve much. He knew that now. It had all been a mistake, his life. And now things were the way they should be. And if he was very, very lucky, someone would be nice to him. Maybe. Someday.

54

Michel lay bleeding, pulsing his life onto the grass. Men ran past oblivious. Then someone stepped on him but he felt nothing. Then other men surrounded him, prodded him, rolled him over and after an argument decided that A) he was not dangerous and B) he wasn't the guy they were after. Michel couldn't speak, couldn't explain any of it to them.

A long time passed before an ambulance pulled alongside Michel and after a discussion about hospitals and insurance, Michel was lifted onto a stretcher and strapped down. The stretcher was tossed into the back of the ambulance. Michel heard the muffled voices from outside the van, heard the stream of police-band radio blather. He wished someone would put a blanket on him. Finally the ambulance rolled off, away from the mall.

A trooper sat across from Michel, saying nothing. He watched Michel warily as if, despite the holes in his body and despite the straps across his legs and chest, he would somehow rise up and tear the trooper apart, only giving the trooper an excuse to put more holes in him. Michel didn't have any fear of the trooper, he let go of emotion altogether. Whatever adrenaline had been coursing through him to give him the courage to go after the man with the gym bag was used up. As the ambulance made the lackadaisical journey to the hospital (no sirens), the last drops of blood leaked out of Michel and stained the stretcher.

But Michel was far away, walking down his road on the way to school. He was trying to see a bird up in the branches of a strangler fig where he could hear it singing. The bird hopped from branch to branch but Michel could only see a tip of wing or tail feather before it would scoot to another branch, deeper and deeper into the foliage of dark leaves. Somewhere a cicada droned.

Michel stopped and began to climb the tree to catch a glimpse of the little bird with the fine voice. The bark was smooth and slippery, but once he got up to the first branch the rest was easy. In amongst the shiny leaves, the warm air hugged him. He lost the bird or any sense of up or down. Then he smelled something. The old dead snake from the road, it was up in the tree and it slithered along a branch toward him. Michel tried to jump, but he could not move. The snake coiled up around his leg and then up around his waist and finally around his chest. Michel was eye to eye with the snake.

As the snake tightened its coils, Michel tried to hold his breath. But the snake gazed into him and Michel saw that the snake was actually Dambala, holding him in his arms. The *loa* understood Michel and all that Michel had been through and was not trying to kill him at all. Only trying to help him find a way out. Michel exhaled and the sky darkened violet and all the leaves around him curled into black paper. Then the black paper became black cloth and then the cloth turned white and fell away as ashes.

It took four attendants in the ER to lift Michel's limp body off the stretcher. Michel had no pulse, no blood pressure at all. He was too comfortable now. His feet had stopped hurting, Marie was making him a chicken sandwich, and so he stayed where he was.

55

Donna had tossed herself from point to point with ease and skill. Full of donuts and coffee and fun and drink and sex she rolled home in Roy's big car. The news reports were nonstop now, everyone realizing this wasn't just any shooting but one that could be talked about for weeks, maybe even make the cover of *Time* magazine. The traffic was bad, but Donna skirted most of it and soon she was floating smoothly along the sylvan two-lane that led back to her kitchen, her furniture, her kid, her husband and her bed.

Thoughts bumped lazily one into another, but no guilt. There were a hundred things she could be doing that were worse than having a few drinks and picking up a skinny, funky teenager. She was a good mother and she was a good wife. Whatever Roy wanted, she did. She couldn't help it if he was a sober stick-in-the-mud. That was his choice.

The Lincoln bounced as it hit first the drainage slant of the street and then the bump of the driveway. The garage door was halfway up as Donna nosed under it, eager to get the big thing in its stall for the night. The purring of the massive car filled the garage, echoing its welcome-home song. Roy had painted a mark on the smooth cement wall to show her when she was "in." She ignored it. She wasn't the one who needed parking lessons.

Roy'd be upstairs in the den, watching TV with the sound down. He would be just a sleepy teddy bear, checking to be sure she got home all right. As far as he knew, things were as she had said they were. If he didn't know the difference, then there *was* no difference.

Randy came panting up to Donna as the garage door ratcheted back down and as she aimed for the steps. "Randy, you stink, you're not coming up. Stay! I'll see you in the morning."

Donna squeezed through the door to the kitchen. The aroma of what Roy and Roy Jr. had had for dinner embraced her like an old friend. Donna wanted a cigarette, but she'd be happy with a few mouthfuls of leftover KFC. She threw her keys on the table, stood by the sink and chewed the rubbery end of a wing. The little yellow plastic floral arrangement Roy's mother had given her on Easter two years ago sat on the window ledge. It was uglier than anything in the world. But the chicken was all right. She flipped off the switch over the sink and the kitchen was almost dark.

Donna stepped toward the glow of light seeping down from the bedroom one split-level above. Her feet touched the wall-to-wall rug. It was nice to be home.

56

Jeff reviewed his options as he watched the immobilized man lying at his feet. He could run and tell the police. He could reach down and grab the pistol and shoot the fucking guy. He could do nothing and wait for the homicidal maniac to wake up and then probably get shot himself. He could start shouting. He could do nothing, wait for the police to find him and the maniac. He could do nothing.

The "do nothing" option repeated in his mind. He was in the middle of an event in his life as complete and dramatic as anything in any piece of literature. This was it. This was being alive. Jeff felt suddenly very clearheaded. Bright light splayed down through the tree branches from a helicopter above. It was only a matter of time before hordes of cops started shooting this place to pieces. The guy was not moving.

"Hey."

The prostrate pile of clothing did not stir.

"Hey, are you alive, dude?"

Jeff stepped closer to the body, which lay face down, an arm outstretched, the pistol gripped in his grimy fist.

"Hey."

Jeff knelt down by the motley head and scrutinized the man's body with care. He thought he could see the back expand with breath, but in the dim light it could have been just an acid ripple in the cosmic skin.

Jeff reached out and gave the shoulder a little shove. Mal clenched his fist and, without looking up, pulled the trigger and a bullet exploded into the leaves and soil. Jeff turned and ran, his decision made.

Huffing, he came to the edge of the trees, where the parking lot began. Jeff stopped and cautiously peered out for police. They were parked out in the lot, a huddle of men behind a seemingly empty couple of patrol cars, the sharpshooters' rifles tripodded on the hoods, trained into the woods to his right. Jeff had no other option. Still breathless, he put his hands up and walked out.

But no one noticed him. He walked out into the parking lot, two hundred feet from where the police sat watching another leg of the woods. When he brought his arms down and turned, he saw a man in Kevlar body armor. The man was walking into the woods led by a leashed Alsatian, also clad in armor. The dog snuffled but did not bark. Jeff stopped and watched as the man and dog disappeared into the tree stand. He turned and walked across the asphalt plain toward the mall.

The fire at the store was extinguished. The fire engines idled nearby as a crew of round-shouldered men pulled plywood and drenched piles of black material out onto the parking lot. Vast puddles of water extended out from the sides of the buildings. Everything was wet, no more flame. Jeff gave them a wide berth and found himself on the walkway that ran around the shuttered mall.

Jeff decided to walk the entire perimeter of the mall one time. If he made it all the way around and didn't see Adelle or Beckett or even Terry, he would go home. Of course, the only pay phones were inside the mall, so he was stuck. As he walked he decided he would cut his dreads off tomorrow. Seriously think about moving away. Pick three books he really liked and take off. Maybe to a small shack in a desert. He'd bring the Bible, *Moby Dick* and *Gravity's Rainbow*. Or maybe just three books by that speed freak who wrote *Through a Glass Darkly*. Dick. Was that his name?

Jeff let his eye travel along the wall as he walked. Exhausted, his mind unraveled to the point where he wasn't thinking anymore, only musing. He heard a gunshot somewhere and wondered whether Mal had shot the cop or the cop had shot Mal. Did it make any difference one way or the other?

Jeff was watching something. At first it seemed like one more shadow along the wall, but in fact, it was someone standing against the wall, in the shadow of the mall gateway Jeff had just now passed. Yes, someone was standing there. Jeff was about to call out when, as he got closer, he could see it was not one but two people embracing, kissing.

Jeff smiled to himself with embarrassment. The phrase *young lovers* flitted through his mind. Two steps closer and he could see the shirt of the taller of the two, the hair and . . . it was Beckett. Beckett was pressing a girl against the wall, his hand under her shirt, a knee between her thighs.

Jeff couldn't see who it was, but he couldn't take his eyes away either. He wanted to walk past unnoticed, but in order to do that he had to walk closer to them before actually passing. He kept moving. They took a breather and the girl, bringing her face into view, over Beckett's shoulder, revealed herself.

Adelle was not shocked to see him. An expression crossed her features, a flattening of the mouth, a slight creasing of her brow. Pity.

Beckett turned, saw Jeff, grunted and continued nuzzling Adelle. Jeff could run back to the woods, find the guy's gun and take care of Beckett right now. He could do that.

Jeff kept walking. He would say nothing. It meant nothing. Whoever she thought she saw, it wasn't him. She didn't know him. He walked onward.

Jeff was trying to be miserable, but the misery wasn't big enough. It wouldn't cover him. He found himself at the next set of large glass doors that led into the mall. These were propped wide open with bundles of newspapers. No one guarded it so Jeff walked in.

The mall was the same, fully lit up but devoid of its warm-blooded content. Jeff knew somewhere in here were police and security men, but he walked on anyway. Past the jelly bean store, the RadioShack, the Ann Taylor, the Victoria's Secret, the toy stores, shoe stores, sporting goods stores, the men's rooms, the women's rooms. Everything locked up and shuttered and as vacant as a church on Monday.

Inside the pet store dirty white puppies lay immobile. Maybe they're dead? Maybe they're stuffed. Jeff grinned to himself, happy with his stoned joke. In the back of the darkened store, Jeff saw the caged parrots. He wondered what they dreamed about. A girl parrot? Freedom? Crackers?

Annoyed by his own poverty of imagination, Jeff ambled on, past the bookstore, past the food court. Looking down the corridor, he saw the yellow tape stretched across the entrance to the wing where the murders had happened. He wondered how long it would take them to reopen that wing. Put in a new store.

What difference did it make? All that thinking and passion and desire to see the big picture was a thing only book people cared about. The people who came to this mall or who drove their cars on the freeway or watched sitcoms didn't care about the big picture or history or literature or any of that. Trying to understand was old-fashioned. There was nothing to understand. The mall was here right now and that was all that counted.

Jeff was infected with a brain disease that forced him to try to make sense of his life. What if sense were only an illusion, a romance of literature, not real at all? The mall was real. Adelle was real. The fire was real. That's all there is, folks. There's nothing behind it. There is no destination to which all this is headed, no progress. Adelle's voice echoed, "And fuck me and stuff?"

Without the friendly polestar of rationality, Jeff wasn't sure he could take another step. You can't believe in what you don't know. And he needed belief. He had fallen off his life raft and it was drifting away. Things didn't make sense and they weren't going to make sense. Things were as they were and it was up to him to get what he needed as best he could. He had seen a dead man tonight. So here he was, empty, walking through an empty, meaningless corridor.

Jeff left the building and began to make his way across the parking lot in the vague direction of "home," the place where his mother was. He would walk in the door and enter a space exactly like the home millions of others lived in.

Jeff moved across the parking lot as substantial as a shadow. A few cars remained, as if abandoned. He passed a car that looked familiar because it was so different.

Immersed in his thoughts, Jeff glanced in without seeing and only after he had walked a dozen more steps did he grasp there was a man in the backseat. Jeff kept walking. If it was a hallucination, there was no need to go back. If it was real, Jeff didn't want to know about it.

But Jeff retraced his steps. There was the guy, looking ill and melted and rumpled. His arms were behind his back and a seat belt was cinched tightly around his middle. His pants were open and his dick was exposed. Jeff tapped on the window.

The guy looked up at Jeff. The eyes were the eyes of a dog who had been beaten by its owner for shitting behind the couch. Jeff tried the door and found it open. A weird stench of urine and body odor wafted out.

"Are you okay?"

Danny didn't answer. He was moving his lips but nothing audible emerged.

"Hey, man, are you okay?"

Danny shivered. "I can't feel my arms. I—"

Jeff stopped him. "Why do you have a seat belt on?"

"So I won't escape. Can you unstrap me?"

Jeff reached forward and flipped the release on the clasp and the belt fell away. The man flopped forward and started moaning. Jeff could see his hands purple with engorged blood.

"How do my hands look? I can't feel them."

"They look kind of swollen. But good. They look good."

"Are you old enough to drive?"

"Of course I am."

"Drive me away from here."

Jeff closed the door, came around the car and got in. The keys were in the ignition. He turned and looked over his shoulder but the man had crumpled down between the back of the front seat and the rear, his knees almost touching the floor. Jeff could hear him sniffling and crying.

"I wet myself. Do you think there's a way to get the handcuffs off?"

Jeff put the car in gear and rolled away toward the exit of the mall. "My father keeps some tools in a shed behind his house. I could probably use something from there."

"Yeah? Your father? Would he be using the tools now?"

"Now? I don't think so. I think he's in bed."

Jeff was greeted with silence from the back.

"Why don't you sleep or something?"

Danny's voice sounded like a child's. "What's your name?"

"Jeff."

"Are you friends with that girl? The one with the green eyes?"

Now it was Jeff's turn not to answer.

"Are you?"

"No. I don't know who you're talking about."

"Good."

There was no way to get home without going up on the highway. The acid was leaking little drip-drops of flashback into Jeff's visual cortex even now. If he focused very hard and gripped the steering wheel with both hands, he could do this. He could drive this guy to his dad's house and get the cuffs off. Then he'd drive the guy home. He'd find his way back to his mom's.

Tomorrow everything would start all over again. He couldn't stop that. Jeff peered through the windshield. He couldn't tell if it was getting lighter out.

Acknowledgments

Thanks to David Rosenthal who said, "Why not?" Thanks to Zoë Wolff for her sharp eye and wit. And thanks to Geoff Kloske for the rigorous final punt. Thanks to my agents, Claudia Cross and George Lane.

About the Author

Eric Bogosian is the author of the plays *Talk Radio, subUrbia* and *Griller* and the Obie Award–winning solo performances *Drinking in America, Pounding Nails in the Floor with My Forehead* and *Sex, Drugs, Rock & Roll,* as well as, most recently, *Wake Up and Smell the Coffee.* He is the recipient of the Berlin Film Festival Silver Bear Award, a Drama Desk Award and two NEA fellowships. An actor who has appeared in more than a dozen feature films and television shows, Bogosian lives in New York City.